Five past midnight...

Thunder rumbled and lightning flickered, closer this time. As he searched each row in the desolate church, electricity danced along Ty's skin, seeming ironic in the powerless city.

He glanced at his watch. Where the hell was Liam? *Unless he never intended to show up.*

He spun and yelled to Gabby, "It's a trap. Get the hell out of here!"

She took two steps before thunder clapped and the building shook around them, the emergency lights going out, plunging the church into blackness.

He heard a crash up ahead, a woman's scream, and his heart jolted in his chest.

"Gabby!" he shouted, but there was no response.

A heartbeat later, the lights flickered back to life.

She was gone.

JESSICA ANDERSEN

MEET ME AT MIDNIGHT

HARLEQUIN®

TORONTO • NEW YORK • LONDON
AMSTERDAM • PARIS • SYDNEY • HAMBURG
STOCKHOLM • ATHENS • TOKYO • MILAN • MADRID
PRAGUE • WARSAW • BUDAPEST • AUCKLAND

Special thanks and acknowledgment are given to Jessica Andersen for her contribution to the LIGHTS OUT miniseries.

To Rebecca York, Rita Herron and Linda Castillo, thanks for being a ton of fun to work with on this four-book series!

ISBN-13: 978-0-373-69279-8
ISBN-10: 0-373-69279-X

MEET ME AT MIDNIGHT

ABOUT THE AUTHOR

Though she's tried out professions ranging from cleaning sea lion cages to cloning glaucoma genes, from patent law to training horses, Jessica is happiest when she's combining all these interests with her first love: writing romances. These days she's delighted to be writing full-time on a farm in rural Connecticut that she shares with a small menagerie and a hero named Brian. She hopes you'll visit her at www.JessicaAndersen.com for info on upcoming books, contests and to say "hi"!

Books by Jessica Andersen

HARLEQUIN INTRIGUE

*Bear Claw Creek Crime Lab

Don't miss any of our special offers. Write to us at the following address for information on our newest releases.

Harlequin Reader Service
U.S.: 3010 Walden Ave., P.O. Box 1325, Buffalo, NY 14269
Canadian: P.O. Box 609, Fort Erie, Ont. L2A 5X3

CAST OF CHARACTERS

Gabriella Solaro—The shy computer science teacher protects her privacy—and her secret—by keeping her online romance strictly online... until her curiosity gets the best of her.

Tyler Jones—As a Secret Service agent and a member of the clandestine black ops group Eclipse, Ty is used to putting missions ahead of his personal agenda. But when he meets Gabby, work and play clash with potentially disastrous results.

Grant Davis—The vice president of the United States of America.

Liam Shea—The electrical expert spent ten years in a military prison for a crime he swears he didn't commit. Now he's out, and he's looking for revenge on the men who ruined his life.

Ethan Matalon, Chase Vickers and Shane Peters—The other three members of Eclipse have each fought their own battles in Liam's mad plan.

Aidan, Finn and Colin Sullivan—Liam's sons each play a vital role in their father's revenge.

Leonore and Tom Wellbrooke—The proprietors of a shelter in South Boston seem like good people, but they have good reason to want the vice president discredited...or worse.

Chapter One

Dear CyberGabby:

I've never used a service like Webmatch.com before, so I apologize in advance if I mess up. I saw your picture and read your profile, and I think we have some things in common. My name is Ty, I'm thirty-five, divorced and relatively free of baggage. Like you, I enjoy classic cars and driving fast. I work as a bodyguard because I also like traveling and staying on the move. It's not as exciting as it might sound, though. I work for a corporate type, so it's mostly standing outside boring meetings. Which, I suppose, is better than actually attending the meetings. Anyway, I'm looking forward to getting to know you better. I've posted my picture and profile (click here). If you're interested, shoot me a note and we can chat.

[Sent by TyJ; March 17, 1:03:13 a.m.]

9:58 p.m., August 2
7 Hours and 40 Minutes to Dawn

Ty Jones paused in the shadows beyond a small, cobbled courtyard in Boston's North End, breathing past the tension of battle readiness.

The light from a kerosene lantern broke the absolute darkness, casting warm shadows on the woman who waited for him in the hot, humid summer night. The lamplight should have been almost painfully romantic.

Instead, it was a necessity.

Boston had been in the grips of a widespread blackout for twenty-five hours now. Most of the city's inhabitants thought there had been a massive failure at Boston Power & Light, but Ty and his teammates knew the blackout had been no accident. It had been a cover. Under the cloak of darkness, a man they'd once trusted had kidnapped Grant Davis, Vice President of the United States.

Now, twenty-five hours later, with Davis's life hanging in the balance and his captor hinting that a bomb had been planted somewhere in the city, Ty and the others were out of time and options.

Which had brought him here, to a clandestine rendezvous with Internet bombshell Gabriella Solaro.

Ty's watch chimed softly. It was ten o'clock. Time to meet the one connection he had left, the one woman who could possibly lead them to Liam Shea, the man behind the blackout.

Taking a deep breath, Ty stepped out of conceal-ment and swung open the ornate wrought iron gate that separated the North End courtyard from the narrow street. Pitching his voice low, he called, "Gabriella?"

The woman was facing away from him. At the sound of her name, she turned and lifted the lantern. "Ty?"

Her voice was soft and feminine, just as he'd imagined it during their online conversations, first in a chat room at Webmatch.com, then one-on-one via e-mail and instant messenger. But oddly, she looked nothing like he'd expected.

Her dark eyes complemented full, red-painted lips, and her features were sharp and exotic, but in the lantern light, her hair seemed darker than the fiery chestnut she'd mentioned, and her simple sundress made her figure seem more angular than her self-de-scribed curvy-bordering-on-plump.

She was lovely, but she wasn't anything like the picture in her profile. Then again, why should that surprise him? It was all too easy to bend the truth and become someone else on the Internet.

He should know.

Stepping forward into the circle of lantern light, Ty hesitated, wondering what she'd expect. Should he hug her? Kiss her? They'd met through an online dating service, which carried a certain expectation, and they'd e-chatted long into many nights, forming the illusion of intimacy. But none of it had been real, had it?

More important, their last few exchanges had been increasingly tense, as he'd pressed for a meeting and she'd resisted, which had solidified his suspicions even before Liam had made his move.

Now, though, Ty had a part to play. He leaned in and kissed her on the cheek. "It's nice to finally meet you in person."

If he hadn't been watching her face as he eased back, he would've missed the moment her eyes slid beyond him to a deeply shadowed corner where two brick-walled houses converged.

Instinct tightened the back of Ty's neck.

Someone was watching.

He forced himself not to react, instead smiling easily. "I'm surprised you agreed to meet me in the middle of this godawful blackout, especially with the curfew and all. Heck, I wasn't even sure my e-mail would get through, or that you'd have enough juice to read it."

With Liam's three accomplices, his sons Finn, Aidan and Colin, all out of action—one dead, one comatose, one not talking—Ty had known Gabby was perhaps their last hope for finding the mastermind. He'd broken into a stranger's car, plugged his handheld into the cigarette lighter and stolen enough charge to send the message. Then he'd waited in the darkness, listening to the sounds of growing violence nearby as the looting continued and the National Guard moved in to enforce the mayor's new curfew. The mob had almost reached him by the time she'd e-mailed back, arranging the meet.

As Ty had locked the car and slipped away for a quick radio convo with his boss, part of him had hoped she'd agreed to meet him out of curiosity, that the woman he'd gotten to know online was the real deal.

Now, as she glanced into the shadows a second time, conflicting emotions stirred within him—vicious satisfaction that he'd come to the right place and disappointment that she hadn't been the real deal, after all.

"I got your message on my Blackberry," she answered. "I was surprised you wanted to meet face-to-face, especially after that last e-mail I sent you, but I was…curious, I guess." She glanced at him, eyes dark and a little cool with an emotion that was either nerves or calculation. "You didn't have any problems getting here? Nobody stopped you?"

"I made it okay." His credentials had gotten him through the first two roadblocks, but he'd ended up ditching his car near the waterfront, where the Guard's bulldozers and tow trucks hadn't yet cleared the roadways. Numerous cars had wrecked right after the blackout, when the traffic lights went down, and even more vehicles had been abandoned later, when rumors of a terrorist attack had sent the city's residents fleeing in panic, only to have them wind up trapped in gridlock, frying in the hot summer sun.

Dull anger kindled in his gut at the thought of so much chaos created by a single ex-con and his sons, but he kept his voice light and friendly when he said, "How about you? No problems so far with the lights off?"

She shifted from one foot to the other, seeming uncomfortable—or was that just part of the act? After a hesitation so brief he wouldn't have noticed it if he hadn't been looking, she tipped her head, fluttered her eyelashes and said, "Would you like to sit down and talk for a little bit? There's a fountain and some benches in the next courtyard over. The neighbors won't mind."

She pointed to a secluded spot where the cobblestone path narrowed between two planted areas, no doubt near where her associate waited.

Keeping his weight evenly balanced on the balls of his feet, ready for a fight, Ty nodded. "The courtyard sounds perfect."

She set the lantern on the edge of a nearby stone planter before starting down the short path. Was it a signal? Ty didn't know, but he was tense with battle readiness as he followed in her wake.

They'd taken just three steps into the shadows when he heard a rustle and the faint indrawn breath that presaged attack.

"Freeze!" Ty palmed the revolver he wore at his hip and grabbed Gabriella in a single move, spinning her back against his body and clamping an arm across her throat.

She screamed and struggled to escape, her elbows digging into his ribs, her heels drumming against his shins. He could feel her heartbeat jackhammering beneath his forearm, mute evidence that she might be a liar, but she wasn't a trained operative.

"Be still." He cocked the revolver, and the click resonated on the humid air, freezing her in place.

He carried a semiautomatic with fifteen in the clip as his primary weapon, tucked into an underarm holster, but he'd long ago found that the six-shooter had the edge when it came to intimidation.

The click said he meant business. Right now his business was finding Grant Davis and locating the bomb that'd been planted somewhere in the city, and to do that, he had to get his hands on Liam Shea.

Adrenaline pounded through Ty's veins as he leaned close and spoke into his captive's delicate ear. "Tell him to toss his weapons and come out with his hands up."

If he was damn lucky, it would be Shea himself. If not, he hoped it was an underling he could lean on for the bastard's location.

Gabby whimpered in the back of her throat and jerked her head in some semblance of a nod. Tears streamed down her cheeks and she was shaking all over, almost enough to convince him she was for real.

A sliver of compassion twisted through Ty, along with snippets from the hundreds of notes they'd exchanged over the past five-plus months. She'd written about honesty, and about problems with her family, and, damn it, she'd seemed real enough that he'd responded in kind.

Maybe she really hadn't known what she was getting into, he rationalized. Maybe it had seemed like a game to her, or perhaps she was one of those bleeding hearts who believed in rehabilitation of hardened criminals.

If so, he could've told her not to bother. Liam had been a traitor eleven years earlier, and he was a traitor now.

One who damn well belonged back in jail.

When there was no motion from the bushes, Ty raised his voice. "Come out here. Now!" A breath of wind disturbed the hot, humid air, unfurling a nearby flag and making it snap. "You've got until three. One…two…"

The bushes moved and a figure stepped out onto the path, nearly lost in the darkness.

"Back up into the courtyard," he ordered, his pulse accelerating as he tried to assess the risks and control the scene.

"Go on. Easy now." He marched Gabby along the path in front of him, using her as a shield as the shadowy figure complied, backing into the courtyard with a hitching motion, as though feeling the way. Moments later, the figure stepped into the circle of lantern light, and the illumination chased away the anonymous shadows.

Ty froze.

It wasn't Liam Shea. It was a woman, and she sure as hell didn't look like anyone's hired gun.

She wore cutoff shorts over curvy legs, with a pink button-down shirt knotted beneath generous breasts. Glossy hair spilled over her shoulders, gleaming with rich chestnut highlights in the yellow lantern light. Her eyes were strangely luminous, as though backlit, bleaching from brown at the center to pale at the edges, and her full, moist lips came straight from his fantasies.

Surprise flared through him, laced with something hotter and even more unexpected. Suddenly desire existed alongside anger, all of it complicated with the pounding need to shelter the innocent and rescue the man he was sworn to protect with his life.

He tried for a dry tone, but the words came out harsh when he said, "Hello, Gabby."

Then he noticed the red-tipped cane in her hand, and saw that she wasn't looking directly at him with those pale, pretty eyes.

A second major shock hammered through him.

Gabriella Solaro was blind.

"LET HER GO, Ty." Gabby knotted her hands together, hoping he wouldn't notice how badly they shook. She couldn't see the scene—her vision was limited to light and dark smudges on the brightest of days—but over the years she'd gotten good at interpreting sights from sounds.

She'd never before had to connect the sound of a weapon to a friend's panicked scream, though, and the reality of it made her sick and dizzy with fear.

This was her fault. Her fault for trying to be someone she wasn't, for thinking she was protected by Internet anonymity, for letting curiosity overrule common sense, for going against everything she'd told him up to this point and agreeing to meet. It was her fault for wimping out and asking Maria to take her place at the last minute. And most of all, it was her fault for being wooed by words on the Braille pinpad she'd designed to translate images from the computer screen to letters she could "see."

Hadn't her friends in the neighborhood warned her about the hazards of online dating? "He could be anybody," they'd said. "He could be a complete jerk. A user. A criminal."

Gabby had brushed them off, figuring she was an expert in dealing with the first two options, and refusing to entertain the third. "I know Ty," she'd said, certain they'd made a connection during their late-night conversations. "He's not like that."

But she'd still refused to take the relationship any further than on-screen…until tonight, when she'd been feeling a little bit reckless, a little bit wild. As usual, the impulses had gotten her into trouble.

Deep trouble.

Heart pounding in her ears, she raised her voice and nearly shouted, "That's right, I'm Gabby."

She was hoping against hope that someone in one of the nearby houses would hear and come help, one of the neighbors she sometimes found overwhelming with their extended Italian-American families and endless dinners, fights and celebrations. But they had ignored curfew and trooped down Hanover Street en masse, banding together to get old Mrs. Rosetti into one of the overflowing hospitals when her oxygen tank ran low and her breathing had gotten bad.

The houses were empty. There was nobody left to hear the tremble in Gabby's voice, or the drum of her heart in her ears. "Please," she said quietly, desperately. "Let her go. I'll do whatever you want."

The offer made her nauseous, but it came from the lessons she'd learned as a teen, when she'd run the streets of Miami with a hard-partying, hard-fighting crowd. She'd fought to outgrow that rebellious, self-destructive streak in the years since, but she needed some of the brashness now, some of that brazen go-to-hell confidence.

She had to get Maria away from him first. Then she'd try to talk him down. She couldn't believe the Ty she'd come to know—

Don't you get it, Gabby? He isn't that Ty. He's... She couldn't even complete the thought. She didn't know *what* he was, or who. All she knew was that she'd brought him into her neighborhood, into her haven. Into her heart.

How she'd agonized over his last few messages, debating how much to tell him, what to tell him. In the end she'd broken up with him rather than admit the truth, that she was blind and rarely left the safe, secure confines of her home territory.

Then he'd caught her in a weak moment with his invitation, and the wild child had taken over and pushed the self-destruct button once again.

"Tell me about Liam Shea," he ordered now, voice low and commanding.

"Let Maria go and I'll tell you anything you want," she countered, gripping her hands tightly in front of her in an effort to hold it together.

Moments later Maria was free. She grabbed Gabby's arm and tried to tug her away, sobbing. "Come on. Please, let's go!"

But Gabby didn't need to see the threat to know Ty hadn't uncocked the gun. He remained in control of the scene.

She pictured him as he'd described himself online—six feet tall and muscular, with blue eyes and blond hair he didn't get trimmed often enough. Her imagination had added a shaggy lock that fell forward over his forehead, along with smile-creases at the corners of his eyes and mouth to counteract the hint of sadness she'd sometimes gotten from his words.

Now in her mind's eye his mouth turned cruel and his eyes glittered ice-cold, sending a shiver of fear through her body.

"Please, Ty," she said quietly. "Let us go. We haven't done anything to you, and we won't tell anyone. Just take the gun and go. I'm begging you. If our conversations meant anything to you, you'll—"

Then she broke off, knowing the conversations hadn't meant anything to him. Not like they had to her. His words had been lies, hadn't they? All lies.

She was surprised, then, when moments later she heard the distinctive click of metal-on-metal, followed by a rustle of nylon cloth and catch of leather as he disarmed the gun and holstered it.

"Tell me everything you know about Liam Shea," he said. "You might know him as Liam Sullivan."

"I don't know anyone by either of those names." Gabby held on to Maria's arm and felt the tension vibrate through her friend, through them both. "Please go. I told Maria's brother to give us ten minutes. He's going to call the police if we don't check in with him by quarter past."

The lie earned her a snort of derision. "Nice try, but we both know the local cops are busy. And besides, I outrank them."

There was another rustle of cloth, and Maria hissed out a breath.

"What is it?" Gabby demanded, trying to ignore a bite of frustration.

"He's with the Secret Service," Maria said, her

Sicilian accent thickening. "Special Agent Tyler Jones," she recited, reading from his ID. "Vice presidential protection detail."

"No he's not," Gabby said, going breathless with shock. "He's a—"

She broke off, realizing that it fit, sort of. "I'm a bodyguard for a corporate type," he'd said, and Grant Davis, a decorated military veteran-turned-golden-boy politician, certainly fit that bill in some respects. Rumor had it he was the front-runner for the next presidential election, and he'd been in Boston this past week for some glitzy affair at the Hancock Building.

Rumor also had it that he'd disappeared right after the blackout.

"Why are you here?" she nearly whispered, fear and confusion stealing her breath. "Why aren't you looking for him?"

"I am," he said bluntly. "I need you to tell me where I can find Liam Shea. If you don't, I'll have no choice but to arrest you as an accessory to the vice president's kidnapping."

The ground pitched beneath Gabby's feet and the world spun invisible circles around her. "I already told you." She swallowed hard when tears pressed at her throat. "I don't know either Liam Shea or a Liam Sullivan. Period, end of discussion."

"You hacked into his Web site on March fifteenth."

"I never—" she began, then broke off, realizing that

her two guilty pleasures—Internet dating and testing her hacking skills against the occasional encrypted Web site—had come to roost simultaneously. And the Secret Service was involved, which meant... *Wait a second*, she thought. *March fifteenth?*

Ty had first e-mailed her through Webmatch.com on the seventeenth. St. Patrick's Day.

Sick humiliation poured through her, nearly dropping her to her knees. "Oh, God. You hit on me because I hacked into this guy's Web site. You—"

She broke off, nausea building when she remembered all the things she'd told him. She might have hidden her blindness and the circumstances leading up to it, but she'd been open about everything else. She'd told him about her growing frustration with the school and the narrow confines of her life, about how she longed for adventure as much as she feared it. In return, he'd urged her to step outside her comfort zone, to embrace life and focus on the people she loved. He'd told how he'd married his high school sweetheart right after leaving the military, and how he heard his retired-colonel father's voice in his head, calming him down when he'd been in tight situations. Or had all that been a lie?

She'd thought they had a connection. It hurt like hell to find out he'd only romanced her because she'd hacked into some guy's Web site.

"Why me?" Her voice cracked on the word and she nearly sagged against Maria.

"Because you hacked into a Web site dedicated to defaming Grant Davis," Ty said coolly.

"Gabby isn't a criminal," Maria said, her accent thickening with anger. "And besides, there must be a hundred Web sites like that."

"Thousands of 'em," Ty agreed. "But this is the only one the vice president asked me to monitor personally. He and Liam…let's just say they have a history."

Gabby's lips trembled. "So you thought that gave you the right to pretend that you—" She broke off, unable to continue.

She might've ended the relationship, but that hadn't prevented her from thinking *What if.* What if they did meet? What if he proved to be a better man than his predecessors, and hadn't minded that she couldn't drive or play golf, and that she sometimes fumbled her way around? What if?

Never once had she thought, *What if it turns out he was only pretending to like me?*

"I'm sworn to protect the vice president with my life," he said. "So, yeah, I'm going to do whatever it takes to keep him safe, including joining a dating service to get close to a woman who hacks through trilevel security like it's nothing."

Maria tugged on her arm. "Let's go. You're not saying another word until you've got a lawyer and this guy's got a warrant or a subpoena or whatever Secret Service agents need."

But Gabby stood her ground, shaking her head. "I don't need a lawyer." She lowered her voice, willing Ty to believe her when she said, "I teach computer science at the Edmunds School. That's a school for the visually impaired, in case your background research on me missed that little tidbit. I visit a ton of Web sites, and yes, sometimes I hack into the more challenging ones, just to prove I can. But that's it. I'm not connected to anyone named Shea or Sullivan, and I have nothing against Vice President Davis. I swear it on my sister's life." She didn't know where that had come from, but although she hadn't seen Amy in over a decade, it was a binding vow. The love remained even though her family had cut her off.

Tears gathered now, welling from the pain in her soul. "As for hacking into encrypted Web sites, you can be sure I've learned my lesson. I won't be Web surfing anymore. You never know what kind of jerk you'll meet."

A tear spilled over and tracked down her cheek when she realized that even though she'd tried to end the relationship rather than meet him in person, some small, unrealistic part of her had hoped for something more when he'd e-mailed earlier, begging for a meeting.

Her voice shook when she said, "Please go."

Ty cursed under his breath and said, "Listen, Gabby—"

But she didn't want to hear his lame excuses, didn't want his pity as the swirling emotions coalesced into a hard, hot ball in her chest and the tears surfaced.

Not wanting him to see her cry, she turned and fled into the darkness.

Ignoring Ty's startled shout, Gabby ran along memorized paths. It was five long steps to the iron gate, twenty across the next courtyard over, then a sharp right-hand turn into the narrow alley between the Robinsons' two-family and Gino Vinzetti's house.

The sounds, smells and shapes of the neighborhood were familiar, grounding her in the realities of her life.

Then footsteps sounded behind her and Ty shouted, "Gabby, wait!"

Sobbing with anger and embarrassment, she hooked a left down Hanover Street, keeping one hand on the rough building faces and using the other to sweep her cane back and forth just in case. She tripped once and nearly fell, but regained her balance and kept going all the way to her apartment, which took up the ground floor of a three-family nestled between a seafood restaurant and a pastry shop.

She was grateful that none of the neighbors were home to see her tears and the way her hands shook when she unlatched the wrought iron gate that led to her side entrance. Hopefully, Ty wouldn't know where she'd gone. She could trust Maria not to tell him.

But he was a federal agent. No doubt he'd known her home address all along.

She blew out a teary breath and let herself inside. She leaned the cane against the door frame, knowing every inch of the apartment without its help, and headed down the entry hall toward the living room, with its soft, embracing couch and familiar, homey smells of cinnamon-scented candles and chocolate chips.

Wanting nothing more than to throw herself onto the couch and scream, she hurried across the room.

Halfway there, she tripped and fell.

Gabby cried out as she slammed her hip into the corner of her coffee table and crashed to the floor. A wave of pain washed through her, radiating from her right hip and elbow.

Dazed, she waited a moment for her head to clear, and then struggled to her hands and knees and felt around. Within moments her fingertips connected with the familiar outline of an antique doorstop cast in the shape of a sailing ship.

A prickle of fear shimmied in her stomach.

The ship was one of a half-dozen iron doorstops she had carefully placed around the apartment. Perhaps they were a strange collector's item for a legally blind person, but she knew where each one was, just as she knew the placement of every wall, every piece of furniture and all the other odds and ends in her space. Everything in her world had its place.

This ship belonged beside the kitchen door, not in the middle of the living room.

Heart pounding, Gabby searched the room by touching each object with trembling fingers. The sofa and coffee table were exactly where they belonged, and nothing else seemed wrong until she levered herself to her feet and felt for the desk. Out-of-place papers crunched underfoot, and there was a blank space where her computer should have been.

"Oh, God." Her throat closed on panic, on denial. "Oh, no. No, no, no. *Please no.*" Her specially outfitted computer, her lifeline to the rest of the world, was gone. Worse, she realized, as she felt frantically along the tabletop, the jumble of half-assembled electronic components was missing, too. She'd been working on a new prototype, a device that could reproduce Web site graphics in three dimensions, allowing blind people to "see" them.

Someone wanted the design, she thought, her mind leaping ahead to seemingly impossible possibilities. *Someone who knew what I was working on, who—*

She spun when she heard the noise. It might have been a quiet cough, or the shift of a shoe on her kitchen tile, she wasn't sure, but she suddenly knew she wasn't alone in the apartment. "Ty?"

"Not exactly," an unfamiliar masculine voice said from the kitchen. She heard footsteps, sensed him move to block the front hallway. "And you can't see me, can you? That'll make this easier than I thought."

The next thing she knew, he was coming straight for her.

Chapter Two

Dear TyJ:
You know how you said the other day that honesty is very important to you? Well then, I'd better be honest with you. I'm not exactly the hotshot computer jockey I made it sound like in my profile, or even in some of our earlier private messages. I teach programming at a small college in the northeast, which is about as exciting as it sounds. As in 'not.' So trust me, the bodyguard gig has me beat by a mile in the 'cool jobs' department, even if you do spend most of your time standing around waiting for something to happen.
[Sent by CyberGabby; April 3, 11:32:32 p.m.]

10:21 p.m., August 2
7 Hours and 17 Minutes until Dawn

Ty stumbled to a halt in the middle of the dark, deserted street and let his flashlight sag, hopelessly lost in the mazelike passageways, courtyards and narrow streets of the North End.

Gabby had outdistanced him easily, moving ghost-like in the darkness. Without backup and an earpiece or, hell, even a functional handheld, he lacked access to the maps and information he normally had at his fingertips.

Which had no doubt been part of Liam's plan.

They'd all learned the theory during Special Forces training—isolate the target and then make the kill. Liam had used the blackout to isolate his former teammates, then he'd moved in for the kill.

He'd sent his sons after those former teammates—Frederick LeBron, Grant Davis, Chase Vickers, Shane Peters and Ethan Matalon. The only unaffected teammate had been Commander Tom Bradley, who'd escaped revenge by dying; the heart attack had taken him before Liam could get to him. LeBron had been in his alpine kingdom in Beau Pays, but the Sheas had gone after his precious daughter, Princess Ariana, and the LeBrons' priceless sapphire. Thanks to Shane, the Sheas hadn't been successful. They'd been equally unsuccessful with Ethan and Chase, whose families had been threatened but returned safely. Still. Liam remained at large, in control of the hostage, Grant Davis, and the bomb.

Ty scrubbed his hand over his face, trying to ignore the feeling that he was running out of time, that he was letting himself get sidetracked. But he couldn't stop flashing back on the look in Gabriella's eyes when she realized why he'd hooked up with her on Webmatch.com.

It wasn't what you think, he'd wanted to say, but he hadn't, because it would have been a lie, and he didn't want to lie to her anymore.

"At least, not if she's telling the truth about Liam," he muttered to himself.

From behind him, a woman's voice said, "You're damned right she's telling the truth."

Even before he turned and shone his flashlight toward the approaching figure, he knew it wasn't Gabby. The voice was too high, and it rolled with strains of Italy.

Maria scowled and crossed her arms over her chest. "She doesn't know anything about your kidnapper, Mr. Secret Service. If she did, she would've told you right up-front. That's the sort of woman she is."

"I need to speak with her," he said. "Please."

She stared at him for a long minute, as though trying to interpret a motivation he couldn't even name. Then finally she gestured with her chin, "Over there. First floor, door's around the side."

"Thanks." He loped across the street, pushed through the wrought iron gate and followed a cobblestone pathway around to the side of a neat, narrow, brick-walled three-family.

His gut tightened when he touched her door and it swung inward. Adrenaline spiked alongside a jolt of concern. Then both were lost as training kicked in and he clicked over to soldier mode. Quiet. Efficient. Deadly.

He left his revolver holstered and pulled the semi-automatic, then flicked off the flashlight. Muscles tense, senses almost painfully alert, he eased through the door, then paused and listened, not sure whether he was walking into an ambush or something else.

The pitch-black inside the apartment made him wish for a pair of night-vision goggles as he eased along, carefully testing each step. Finally he cursed and clicked on the flashlight, using his fingers to muffle the glow and let only a small beam shine through.

He uttered a low curse when he saw the condition of her apartment, and the scale tipped away from ambush ever so slightly.

A doorway to his left opened onto a small kitchen, where the refrigerator door hung open, its contents in disarray. A head of lettuce had rolled beneath a small butcher-block table; most of the cabinet doors and drawers were open; and the single counter held a jumbled mess of papers and canned goods.

The kitchen wasn't just messy, Ty thought on a bite of rage. It'd been tossed, and by someone with a temper.

The back door off the kitchen hung open. Was it a sign that the intruder had gone, or was it set up for a quick getaway? He didn't know, and that worried him more than it should have, making him wonder about a woman who'd hacked into a murderer's Web site but claimed it was on a lark, a woman who just happened to live in the same city where the kidnapping had gone down, yet professed innocence. It just didn't play, he told himself yet again. There were too many coincidences for her to be innocent.

Problem was, he was starting to think she was exactly that.

Gut tight, he checked the kitchen closet and glanced out into the alley. There was no sign of the intruder. There was also no sign of chestnut hair and feminine curves. Where the hell was she?

Refusing to consider the worst-case scenario until he'd thoroughly searched the place, he worked his way back through the kitchen and further into the small apartment.

Three more doors opened off the narrow hallway. The first led to a closet; the second opened into a sitting room.

The desk was in shambles, and an expensive-looking computer and an array of electronics lay in the corner, smashed to pieces. Oddly, though, the TV and the high-tech sound system appeared untouched.

This wasn't a burglary, then. But what exactly was it? And why?

Though the timing seemed coincidental—there was

that word again, *coincidence*—Ty shoved his gathering suspicions aside and focused on the priority, which was finding Gabby and making sure she was okay.

Tension hummed through him as he eased toward the last of the three doorways. He flashed back on the moment after the blackout, when the emergency lights had come up at the John Hancock building to reveal a party in shambles, the president and vice president missing. Though President Stack had been found nearby, drugged and confused, VP Davis had not.

Had Gabby been taken hostage, as well?

There'll be hell to pay if she has, he thought out of nowhere, as he eased through the last door into her bedroom.

There he hesitated for a half second before letting the flashlight beam play over her bed. Unlike the other rooms, which he noted, were devoid of color this room was vibrant. The king-size bed had a fluffy duvet draped with a woven afghan in the deepest of jade greens, and pillows of every shape and size formed a drift against the plush, padded headboard, all in vibrant jewel tones visible even in the wan illumination.

It was, he realized, as unexpected heat burned through his veins, almost exactly as he'd imagined it during their online "dates." He let his gun hand sag—

And the moment of hesitation nearly cost him everything.

A blur came at Ty from the side. He turned and

ducked in a single motion, and the blow glanced off his shoulder. His attacker cursed and kicked out, sending Ty's gun and flashlight spinning away.

The light smashed into the wall, plunging them into darkness. The gun clattered somewhere off to their left, momentarily lost.

Ty lunged for the other man and they went down on the floor beside Gabby's bed. "Where is she?" he grated, landing a gut punch that had the other guy wheezing. "Where is Grant Davis? If you've hurt either of them, I'll kill you."

A blow caught Ty at the temple. His head snapped back, and he saw stars where there weren't any. Fury spiked. Roaring, he grabbed for the bastard, got a fistful of his shirt and punched him hard in the face. The impact bruised his knuckles and sang up his arm.

"You want to get back to basics?" he grated. "How's this for basic?" He landed a second punch and thought he felt bone give.

The other man went limp. An atavistic thrill ran through Ty, a surge of victory, of rage. He shifted his grip and reached for the handcuffs he wore on his belt.

With a roar, his opponent exploded into action beneath him, reversing their position and driving his fist into Ty's jaw.

He saw stars again.

Then blackness.

BREATH SOBBING in her lungs, Gabby tugged at the bars on her bathroom window. When she'd first rented the place, she'd considered them a necessary security measure.

Now they were a trap.

She heard another crash in the bedroom, followed by a pained shout from a second man. She thought it was Ty's voice, but how could she be sure? She'd barely met him.

"Come on," she hissed, and yanked at the unyielding bars again, knowing it was futile but unable to make herself stop trying. *"Come on!"*

Behind her, beyond the bathroom door, the fighting sounds abruptly cut off.

Gabby froze. She strained to hear what was happening out there, needing to know who'd won.

She heard only silence, followed by the sound of footsteps in the bedroom.

Ty would've called her name, right? He would've said something to let her know he was okay.

Unless he wasn't okay.

No, Gabby thought as the footsteps paused and she heard the sound of her closet door opening and clothes hangers being slid aside on their metal bar. *Oh, no.* Her fingers fell away from the window grate and her throat clenched until only a trickle of oxygen got through.

The footsteps resumed, drawing nearer.

A weapon. She needed a weapon.

Nearly wheezing with fear, she groped near the wall until her fingers found a smooth plastic shaft, like a length of pipe. She closed her fingers and tested its weight, then decided it would have to do.

A click of metal on metal signaled the turn of the bathroom knob. Gabby braced herself and raised her weapon.

The door opened. She screamed as loud as she could, and attacked. She lunged toward the sound and swung, yelling, "Get out of my house, you bastard!"

Her first blow missed the intruder and slammed into the wall. The impact sang up her arms and numbed her fingertips, but she couldn't stop now. When she heard a rustle of cloth and felt motion nearby, she yelled again and swung.

This time she connected with flesh. She felt the blow land, heard a man curse.

Then he grabbed her, banding one strong arm around her torso and clapping the other across her mouth. "Shh! Quiet. Knock it off!"

She swung and connected with the back of his head. He swore and shook her. "What is wrong with you? Can't you see—" Then he broke off. "It's Ty, Gabby. It's Ty. You're okay."

He repeated the reassurance a few more times, but she'd already stopped struggling, letting herself go limp in his grasp as his words played through her mind. *Can't you see?*

No, I can't, damn it. Anger spurted—at him, at whoever had broken into her house, her sanctuary. But beneath the heat of rage was another warmth—the feeling of being held in a man's arms. In Ty's arms.

That last thought shouldn't have mattered. He'd lied to her, damn it. He'd used her emotions to pursue a lead. It hadn't been about romance for him. It'd been the job.

Trouble was, her body didn't seem to care.

"Shh," he whispered against her temple, his breath ruffling her hair. "I think he's gone, but I'm not positive. I needed to make sure you were okay before I went after him."

They were pressed back to front, with the solid wall of his chest braced against her shoulders, the strong columns of his thighs touching intimately against the backs of hers.

Seeming to realize it, he shifted away and loosened his grip on her body. "You done screaming?"

She nodded against the hand that still covered her mouth. When he released her, she said, "Sorry, I thought you were…whoever that was."

"I know. Lock yourself in here while I search the house."

"Wait." She put out a hand and touched his forearm, which was warm and solid beneath a layer of cotton shirt. "Does this mean you believe that I'm not involved with the man you're looking for?"

There was a long pause before he said, "I haven't

decided yet." Then he exhaled. "The mess out there certainly strengthens your case, except for two things."

"What things?"

He turned away from her, distance muffling his voice. "For one, I don't get how he'd know to toss your place while we met, unless he knew about the meeting."

"Maybe he was following you," she said, but that wouldn't have worked with the timing. "Even better, maybe he's monitoring your e-mail." She shrugged. "I could do it." Right about now she was wishing she'd back-hacked his account and taken a look. It would've saved her a little bit of heartache and a whole lot of embarrassment.

It might've saved her computer, too. If she'd told him to take a hike when he first started e-mailing her…she would've missed some very good times, she admitted, and hated him for the truth of it.

Why couldn't he have been the man he'd pretended to be?

"We can talk about it later," he said, and for a moment she thought he meant they could talk about the so-called romance they'd conducted. Then she realized he was talking about whether she was involved in the vice president's kidnapping, and reality returned with a vengeance.

Her house had been ransacked. She'd been chased into her own bathroom. Ty had been attacked in her bedroom. For all they knew, their attacker was still out there.

"Take this." She pressed her bludgeon into his hand.

There was a short pause, then a snort. He returned the weapon, and there was a thread of laughter in his voice when he said, "I've got a gun. You keep the toilet plunger."

TY'S AMUSEMENT was short-lived, though. Once he was back out in Gabby's bedroom, sweeping the flashlight to make sure he hadn't missed anything, he was all business. He wasn't thinking about the blazing fury that'd pounded in his chest as he'd struggled with the intruder, or the way Gabby's curves had felt nestled against him.

Or if he was thinking those things, he shoved them deep inside, where the emotions couldn't distract him from the most important things, couldn't deflect him from the job.

"Where are you, Liam?" he said quietly as he worked his way out of the bedroom and back down the hall, retracing the path he'd taken only minutes earlier, though it felt like he'd aged a year in that brief space of time when he'd thought Gabby was gone.

Focus, Tyler, his father's voice said in Ty's head. *Keep your mind in the game.*

And though Colonel Jones had been speaking about high school sports, and the words had come long before Ty had followed family tradition by enlisting, the advice held true now.

It was past time for Ty to focus on his priorities—finding Liam, liberating Grant Davis and neutralizing the bomb threat. It wasn't about the woman. It had, quite possibly, never been about her.

Ty searched the house, flashlight and gun both held at the ready, but there was no sign of the intruder, and the streets outside were dark and deserted.

Convinced the place was clear, he returned to the ransacked bedroom and knocked quietly on the bathroom door. "Gabby? It's okay. You can come on out. I need to ask you a few questions." Like what was missing. Who she thought had been in her house.

And why the break-in had coincided with their rendezvous in a courtyard down the street.

The door opened and Gabby stood at the threshold for a moment, lit by the warm yellow beam of his flashlight. Her chin was up and defiant, her pale eyes clear. That, coupled with her lovely hair, which gleamed even in the feeble light, combined to make her seem ethereal. Magical. More, somehow, than the woman he'd imagined during their late-night conversations, when the line between lies and reality had begun to blur.

Focus!

Ty scowled. "Look, I think we need to get something straight here. I never—"

The digital ring of his handheld interrupted, surprising him. He'd thought the battery too low to grab a signal, not to mention the lack of cell coverage twenty-five hours into the blackout.

Figuring it was Chase, Shane or Ethan with new information, he flipped the phone open, welcoming the faint blue glow. The four of them comprised Eclipse, an under-the-radar black ops group that had grown out of their military service. Work with Eclipse had taken them to every hellhole on the globe and made them the best of friends. The kind you trust with your life.

It took Ty a moment to realize it wasn't a call, then another moment to read the text message in the fading glow of the dying battery.

"Nice punch. You got lucky, but your luck is about to change. If you want to see Grant Davis alive, bring your girlfriend and meet me at midnight at the O—"

That was all he got before the battery quit.

GABBY HEARD his hiss of indrawn breath, and immediately tensed. "What is it?"

"It is, or rather *was*, a text message." He repeated it aloud, not bothering to hide his irritation, or the way his voice went dry on the word *girlfriend*.

Hey, she wanted to tell him, this isn't my fault. Which made her realize that the reverse was true. Anger flared in her chest and she snapped, "That guy broke in because of you, didn't he? Because he saw us together."

"Maybe," he said neutrally. "Or maybe you and he were working together and something backfired."

"Don't be stupid." Her breath hissed between her teeth. "I didn't ask you to come here. In fact, I'm pretty sure I tried to end it between us. I would have been perfectly happy never meeting you in person." Or if not happy, at least content. Safe and secure in her little world, which no longer seemed quite so safe. "This man—Liam was it? He came here because of you. He wrecked my things. He took my computer, for God's sake. Do you know how much that thing cost me, and how long it's going to take me to rebuild the Braille translation hardware? I'd finally gotten the peripherals exactly where I wanted them." She broke off, aware of his silence and nearly palpable tension. "And you don't care about that, do you?"

He exhaled. "Your stuff isn't stolen, but it's busted up pretty good. And it's not that I don't care, it's that I have bigger things to worry about right now."

"Vice President Davis," she said, remembering the text message and trying not to linger on the word *girlfriend* or think about how long it'd been since that word had applied to her for real. "Do you know where you're supposed to meet this guy?"

She could feel him weighing his answer. Finally she heard him shift and give heard a low curse. "No, I don't. And it's nearly midnight, damn it."

That surprised her. Hadn't it just been ten o'clock?

Hadn't she just been hiding in the corner of the court-yard, unable to bypass the opportunity to meet Ty, even if only through Maria's eyes?

Apparently not. Apparently nearly two hours had passed in a blink.

"Let's work this through logically," she said, thinking fast. "He was just here and he knows you and I are here. That suggests the meeting place is some-where nearby."

He didn't speak for a minute, and she'd just about decided he wasn't going to answer her at all when he suddenly said, "How many places within, say, a five-minute walk have names that begin with the letter *O?*"

She thought fast, partly to help, partly to make him go away, make it all go away so she could lock her doors and crawl back into her familiar, comfortable patterns. "There are a couple of restaurants that begin with *O*—Orsini's and Only Seafood. But they're closed because of the blackout."

"Not a restaurant," Ty said. "He thinks bigger than that. Something important. A monument, or an histori-cal building, maybe?"

"Let me think." She frowned, reviewing her mental map of the area. She imagined herself walking up one street and down the next, counting the steps, tapping with her cane. At the edges of her brain, a faint sensory memory lingered. It was the smell of old wood and candle wax, overlain with the fragrance of summer flowers. It could've come from a hundred places in the historical city, but this impression brought a sense of peace. Of reverence. "There's a big church nearby, but it's called Christ Church."

"Which doesn't start with an *O*," he said.

"No, but that's not its only name." Excitement built as the connection clicked in her brain. "They used to call it the Old North Church."

"As in 'one if by land, two if by sea'?" he quoted. "That Old North Church? I thought it was near the water."

"We are," she countered. Realizing he didn't know the city well, she led him to the front door. It hung open, letting in the night air, which was heavy with summer humidity and the hint of an incoming squall. She gestured beyond the neighborhood, nearly due east. "The New England Aquarium is that way, right on the harbor." She turned and pointed northwest. "The church is that way, overlooking the mouth of the river. Two blocks over, one up. You'll make it if you run."

"*We'll* make it," he corrected. "Come on."

"Not on your life." Heart picking up a beat, Gabby backpedaled up a step and reached for her front door, for safety. "I've had more than enough excitement for tonight. You're on your own."

But when she swung the panel shut, he blocked it halfway. "The message said to bring my girlfriend."

"I am *not* your girlfriend," she snapped.

"He doesn't know that. If you're innocent, then

you're right—he either followed me and backtracked you to your place somehow, or he already knew about you from my e-mails. Now he's wondering exactly how much you know, or how important you are to me." He paused. "Either way, you'll be safer with me than staying here." His words sounded logical, but there was an undercurrent in his tone that she didn't like.

Swallowing past the growing knot of panic in her throat, Gabby shoved on the door, trying to force it closed. When he resisted, they engaged in a brief tussle that brought tears of frustration to her eyes. "Would you just go!" she shouted. "Go away and leave me alone! I'm not the person you're looking for!"

Her words echoed, gaining new meaning.

Ty's voice went soft. "Listen, Gabby—"

"No, you listen," she said, her temper spiking. "I joined Webmatch because I was looking for a friend. Someone who doesn't need much sleep, like me. Someone I could talk to." Her voice broke on the memory of the things they'd said to each other during their nighttime exchanges, things she'd never told anyone else. Things that made her feel stripped bare now. "I wasn't looking to become part of some shoot-'em-up that belongs in an action movie, not real life!"

But even as she said that, a small part of her wondered whether she might not have been looking for adventure, after all. Something new and different. A way out of her rut. A hint of danger amidst the peace.

Why else had she discouraged all the other respondents and homed in on a divorced bodyguard who, by his own admission, rarely stayed in one place too long and dated online because his lifestyle didn't leave room for a more traditional relationship?

Typical, she thought with a burst of self-directed anger. *Just typical.* Whenever she had things running smoothly in her life, that same little destructive part of her had to step out and mix things up by goading her into doing things she knew she shouldn't.

"I know this situation really, really stinks," Ty said. "But I need your help. Hell, it may sound corny, but your *country* needs your help. This guy is serious, Gabby. If I don't follow his instructions to the letter, he could kill the vice president. He's made that clear before, with my partners. Are you willing to risk Grant Davis's life?"

She sucked in a breath. "That's not fair."

"Nothing about this is fair." His flat tone warned her that there was more to the story than he was letting on. "But that doesn't change the fact that I need you to come with me." His voice dropped, turning persuasive. "Come on, take my hand. I'll make sure nothing bad happens to you."

She could hear the lie in his voice. He was afraid for her, maybe a tiny bit afraid of her, afraid that she'd turn the tables on him. But he was also a Secret Service agent sworn to protect the vice president. Just how far would he go to follow that oath?

Close the door, said the logical, practical self she'd worked so hard to cultivate, even as the rebellious, frustrated part of her said, *Go with him, he needs your help.*

A sinking pit opened up in the bottom of her stomach as she made the decision. "Okay. I'll go."

"Thank you." She could feel him shift toward her, as though he was going to touch her, then he hesitated and drew away. "We're going to need to move fast and keep out of sight," he warned. "Curfew started at dusk, and I don't want to attract any more attention than necessary. Stay close to me and be ready to move if I say to."

Again his words held an undercurrent that made her long to see his face, so she could tell what was real and what was a lie.

She thought about changing her mind. Instead she grabbed her cane, stepped outside and closed and locked the door to her ransacked apartment. "Let's go." When he moved to take her hand, she shook him off. "I'm fine."

It wasn't until he'd stumbled for the third time that she realized his flashlight batteries must be dying or already dead. Without a word she reached over, took his hand and led him into the darkness.

Chapter Three

Gabby:
I'm sorry if I was being too pushy the other night on Instant Messenger. I'm not the jealous sort, honest. I wasn't asking about other guys to go all *Fatal Attraction* on you, either. It's just that I know there's got to be a reason you're home alone every night, and I want you to know that I'm here if you want to talk about whoever hurt you. If you want to talk about anything, really, I'm here for you.
[Sent by TyJ; April 15, 1:30:00 a.m.]

11:50 p.m., August 2
5 Hours and 48 Minutes until Dawn

The streets and buildings were ghosts, the blackness nearly absolute, broken here and there by kerosene and propane lanterns, along with the occasional battery-powered fluorescent lamp, though Ty had noticed the latter growing increasingly scarce as the blackout moved into its second full night.

The overall effect was one of being transported back in time. He could've been walking the cobblestone streets back when Paul Revere had ridden to warn the militias that the British were coming, and the Colonies had teetered on the brink of war. Now, as Ty followed Gabby down the street, he felt as though he were back in a war zone himself. Not in the messy conflicts of the Middle East where he'd first met Liam, but in a far more private war among soldiers.

"*Revenge*," Ethan had said. Liam wanted revenge on the men who'd been part of the hostage rescue op that had cost him his career and reputation.

But it didn't play quite right for Ty; kidnapping and wholesale slaughter seemed out of character for the man he remembered.

Back then, Liam had been an electrical expert, an officer who'd risen quickly through the ranks due to his intelligence and skills, along with the undeniable benefit of coming from a wealthy family of Irish immigrants turned military men and politicians. He'd been the golden boy, the one who'd seemed inevitably destined for greatness. Instead he'd fallen to dishonor.

He'd spent ten years in a military prison, but Ty still found it difficult to reconcile the man he'd known with the kidnapping and the bomb threat. More personally, he couldn't square it with the things Liam and his sons had done to the other members of their Special Forces team. Liam's sons hadn't just attacked Frederick, Shane, Chase and Ethan; they'd attacked their families and the people they loved.

Lucky for Ty, he didn't have a loved one anywhere near the Boston area. The colonel and his mother were safely entrenched in the Maryland town where Ty grew up, and love hadn't been on his radar screen for quite some time.

As they passed a house that glowed with more lights than the others, he glanced over at Gabby, weathering the punch of lust that had hit him the moment she'd stepped out of the shadows and faced him down, and hadn't died yet.

Whether or not she was an innocent—and the jury hadn't come back on that one—she was lovely. Her porcelain skin held a hint of color over her cheekbones, and the soft waves of her hair framed her oval face in a style that was simultaneously classic and modern. A style that made him want to reach out and touch.

She must have heard him turn his head, or maybe she'd sensed the weight of his stare, because she glanced over. Their eyes met, and though he knew she couldn't see him, there was an almost palpable connection.

"You're nothing like I expected," he said before he thought to guard his speech.

Her lips twitched, but there was no humor in her faint smile. "At least we've got that much in common." She paused. "For what it's worth, I liked the guy you pretended to be."

"He liked you, too," Ty said. But he didn't bother to pretend he was that guy.

When he saw a shadow darken her pale eyes, he was tempted to apologize, to explain, to let her know that some of it had been real for him, too.

Instead he looked away. What was the point? Even if they'd met under other circumstances, he never would have followed through.

"Come on," he urged. "It's nearly midnight."

Five more minutes of walking brought them to a towering church made of brick and trimmed in white wood. High above them a white steeple rose up and was lost in the darkness. Windows were set at regular intervals, glowing with faint light.

His watch chimed midnight.

He guided her up the steps to the arching main door and pulled his weapon as he followed close behind. "Please tell me it isn't locked."

She shook her head and said quietly, "It's one of the few buildings in the neighborhood with a generator. The reverend said he'd leave it open until the lights come back on, though with the curfew I doubt there's anyone here. The National Guard came through earlier this evening, moving people to temporary camps if they didn't have anywhere else to go. I guess they were afraid the looting might spread up to this area before long."

Twenty-seven hours into the blackout, Ty thought, *and Boston's turning into a war zone.*

The heavy door swung inward to reveal a spacious lobby with several sets of glass-paned doors beyond. Ty led the way through and swept the area beyond with his weapon.

Part of him took in the neat double row of wooden pews and the gloriously soaring columns on each side, leading to balconies that faded into the darkness. The emergency lights glinted on an ornate double chandelier and on the cloth-draped altar and pulpit. But even as he noted the dimly lit details, another part of him searched the shadows.

The church seemed deserted.

"Stay close," he said quietly. He took Gabby's hand and hooked her fingers into his waistband, leaving his own hands free. He started down the aisle with her in tow, and he tried like hell to block the memories of the last time he'd been in an actual church, the last time he'd walked down an aisle.

His damned wedding.

Focus. He scanned each row of seats but saw nothing out of place. He strained to detect the sounds of an ambush but heard no footsteps, no quiet breathing. They had just about reached the end of the aisle when his flashlight quit for good. He muttered a curse and tucked it in his pocket in case he found more batteries or needed something to throw.

Without warning, lightning lit the scene, a triple flash that came strobe-bright. Ten seconds later thunder rumbled, deep-throated and loud, though still some distance away.

"That's going to complicate things," he muttered under his breath, knowing that an electrical storm would only make things tougher for the National Guard, and for the teams struggling to fix the power plants Liam had sabotaged in order to trigger the blackout.

Lightning flickered again, closer this time, and electricity danced along Ty's skin, seeming ironic in the powerless city.

He glanced at his watch. Five past midnight. Where the hell was Liam? He was the one who'd arranged the meet in the first place.

Unless he never intended to show up, Ty thought on a jolt of adrenaline.

He spun and yelled, "It's a trap! Get the hell out of here!"

Lightning flashed again, showing him Gabby's quick comprehension, her panicked bolt. She took two steps toward the door before the thunder clapped and the building shook around them.

The emergency lights went out, plunging the church into Stygian blackness.

"Keep going!" he shouted as he stumbled and nearly fell. "I'll be right behind you!"

He heard a crash up ahead, a woman's scream, and his heart jolted in his chest.

"Gabby!" he shouted, but there was no response.

A heartbeat later, the emergency lights flickered back to life.

She was gone.

GABBY STRUGGLED, but her attacker—big and solid and male—held her pinned by her throat and one arm, helpless. She tried to scream, but he kept a hand across her mouth, muffling her cries as he dragged her up a flight of stairs. Knowing she had to make some sort of noise to attract attention and let Ty know where she was, she kicked out, slamming her sandal-clad feet into the wall so hard pain sang up her legs.

Over the pounding of her heart, she heard Ty's shout. "Gabby!"

She yanked in his direction and managed to wrench away from her captor's muffling hand. "Ty! I'm up here!"

She wrenched the rest of the way free and bolted back toward the stairs, toward Ty's voice, but without the help of her cane she tripped and went down on her hands and knees. Sobbing, she scrambled back to her feet and turned to run.

For the second time that night, the click of a revolver froze her in place.

"You don't want to do that." The stranger's voice was cool and distant and held a faint New England accent overlaid with something hard and harsh. "Over there. Sit down." When she didn't move, he cursed under his breath, grabbed her arm and shoved her onto a hard wooden pew.

Then he raised his voice and called, "I've got your vice president and your woman now, Ty. I'd say the score's two-nothing in my favor."

"This is no game, Liam." Ty's voice seemed closer now, though it still came from down below, on the first floor. "Give it up before anyone else gets hurt." His tone dropped, became cajoling. "You don't want to do this. Think about it."

Gabby's captor gave a bark of laughter. "Stuff it, Ty. I've done nothing *but* think about this for the past ten years. What else does a man do in prison except make plans for when he gets out?"

Prison. Gabby's breath escaped from between her lips on a moan and her head spun. She jammed her fist in her mouth and bit down, both to stop another cry and to keep herself from fainting.

"Let the woman go," Ty answered. "She's done nothing to you."

"She apparently means something to you, though, and that's enough," Liam answered. Cloth rustled as he shifted his stance, mere feet away from Gabby.

Moaning, she slumped back in the pew, then let

herself fall until she was lying on her side with her face pressed into the polished wood of the hard bench. When the tears tried to come, she let them fall, feeling the wetness course down her face.

Liam cursed under his breath and nudged her with the gun. The cool metal poked her in the ribs as thunder clapped in the near distance. Electricity danced in the air, raising the hairs on her arms and making her want to shiver.

"I've taken care of the others," Liam said. "Shane, Chase, Ethan…they've gotten what's coming to them. Now it's your turn."

Gabby's stomach fisted. She didn't know the men, but if he'd already killed so many, he might not hesitate to add two more to the tally.

"If I'm the one you want, then take me," Ty said. "Let the vice president and the woman go."

"You know better than that." Liam's voice dimmed slightly, as though he'd turned away. "I've had years to plan this, years spent in prison for something I didn't do. To balance the scales, I'm aiming to hit each of you where it hurts—except Bradley. Our commander," he said the word with disdain, "is already dead. But I'll get the rest of you. Shane loses his reputation as a security expert. LeBron loses his precious sapphire. Chase loses his girlfriend and their baby, Ethan his wife and son. But you? You've already lost your wife, haven't you, Tyler? What can I do to hurt you besides make you responsible for the death of the man you've idolized for nearly half your life?"

"If you kill Grant Davis…" Ty began, his voice nearly a growl.

"I won't kill him," Liam said. "You will, if you don't find him in time. You remember your part in our little op, don't you? Think of it that way, only in reverse. This time instead of setting the bomb as a diversion so we can get the hostages out, you're going to have to find and defuse the bomb before it blows your precious vice president all over Boston." He chuckled. "Not to mention the part where it takes out a good chunk of the city in the process."

The words chilled Gabby with their violence and the mad logic of his tone, but the timbre of his voice had grown muffled, indicating that, believing her unconscious, he'd swung his attention away from her in order to play to a crowd of one, grandstanding into the darkness.

Knowing this might be her only chance, she eased herself off the pew and crept along the row, away from Liam's voice. Rather than cursing her blindness—the time for that was long past—she focused on the things she could perceive, like the smooth wooden pew edge on one side of her, the carved pew back of the next row over, the smell of candle wax and incense, and the echoes surrounding her. When Liam continued his taunts, she moved faster, hoping against hope that he wouldn't turn and see her escaping.

"Of course, it won't be as simple as that," Liam continued, though Ty hadn't said anything. "Remember those planning sessions with Commander Bradley? Remember how he said an op was like a treasure hunt, and it was up to us to track down all the clues necessary for success? Well, now it's up to you to find all those clues."

This time when Liam paused and Ty still didn't respond, Gabby knew she had to move faster. Heart pounding in her ears, she stood and ran, keeping one hand on the line of pews for guidance.

Behind her, Liam cursed viciously, the sound sharpening as he turned to face her. "Hold it right there!"

Gabby ducked her head and ran, feet nearly skidding on the wooden floor. She reached the end of the pew line and hooked a left, letting her hand skim over the edges of the rows as she fled down the short aisle to where the stairs must be.

"Stop!" Liam shouted. Moments later gunfire cracked, echoing in the sacred halls of Christ Church.

Glass shattered next to Gabby's head. She screamed, lunged forward—

And stepped into thin air.

Arms windmilling, she overbalanced and fell, slamming her hip into the stair railing as Liam fired a second shot. She caught a toe on the next stair tread and went down, tumbling headfirst into the warm, unyielding bulk of a man's body.

Ty's body. She knew him instantly, though she couldn't have said how or why.

He grabbed her by the arms, steadying her on her feet. "Come on!" He pulled her down the stairs at a run, his grip both hurrying her and holding her up when she stumbled. Heart pounding, she hung onto his arm and followed his lead.

They hit the end of the stairs and headed for the lobby and the main doors beyond. She judged them halfway across the great hall when Liam's voice boomed down from above. "Think about it, Ty. If you leave, you won't know where to start looking for your precious vice president...or for the bomb."

Cursing, Ty spun them and shoved Gabby behind a set of heavy doors that separated the great hall from the lobby.

"Stay there!" he hissed, and then his footsteps moved away a few paces.

He was trying to draw Liam's fire, she realized. Trying to protect her while playing Liam's game in order to find the vice president and the bomb.

She should have hated Ty for what he'd done to her, for how he'd played on her emotions and made her think he cared. Instead, in that moment, she felt an unexpected flicker of respect. An unwanted stir of excitement.

"Tell me where to start looking," he said calmly. "This is your game, Liam. Your rules."

A roll of thunder punctuated his words, and the air

hung heavy with a sense of anticipation, as though the storm was crouched atop the city, waiting for some unknown signal.

"You're damn right I make the rules, and rule number one is that nothing in life is free. You give me the woman and I'll tell you where to find Davis."

"Not an option," Ty said flatly. "You want me to play your game? You want revenge for whatever I did or didn't do eleven years ago? Then let the woman go free, and I'll play."

The only answer was a low, angry mutter of thunder.

Ty cursed, then called, "That's my only offer. Take it or leave it."

"I think not," Liam answered from very nearby, making Gabby gasp in shock. Just as Ty had done earlier, Liam had used the storm to cover his movement as he shifted position. He was on the first floor now, somewhere opposite Ty just inside the great hall.

Liam continued, "You're a demolition man, Ty, not a negotiator. So I'll say it one last time before the deal's off the table. You give me the woman and I'll tell you how to find Grant Davis." He paused. "Think about it. You'd be trading a nobody for the vice president of the United States. A man you've sworn to take a bullet for. How is that a bad bargain?" Liam paused again, and his voice took on a note of sly calculation. "Unless she's not a nobody. You tell me, Ty. Just how much do you know about Gabriella Solaro?"

Gabby froze, her heart lunging into her throat. Ty hadn't called her by name, so how did Liam know who she was?

Ty went silent, no doubt wondering the same thing. She could sense his tension, feel the battle inside him. Or was that just wishful thinking?

"Fine," he said abruptly. "Take her."

Before she could react, before she could run for the door and scream for help, Ty closed on her, grabbed her by the upper arm and tugged her further into the church. He shoved her, sending her stumbling forward three paces. She banged into the corner of a pew and cried out, then shrieked again when fingers closed tightly on her arm.

"Shut up," Liam said, his voice inflectionless. Then she felt him shift against her as he turned back to Ty. "Follow the campaign trail."

There was a pause before Ty said, "Explain."

"No," Liam said, and pressed his weapon to Gabby's head. "Now, if you're half as smart as I remember, you'll start running. You have until dawn. Sunrise is at 5:38 a.m. You might want to set your watch, because you're going to get a hell of a show. Unless, of course, you manage to find and defuse the bomb."

It wasn't until Gabby heard Ty's receding footsteps that she realized he wasn't planning on rescuing her.

No, he'd handed her over for real. And he was leaving. *Wait!* she wanted to shriek. *What about me?* But she didn't dare because of the gun pressed to her temple, and because of the burgeoning fear that he wouldn't turn back even if she did cry out.

Instead she whispered, "Ty." A tear spilled over as the image of an Internet lover shattered in her heart, and she realized she'd done the dumbest thing possible—she'd fallen for a man who didn't exist.

"Come on." Liam uncocked the revolver and put it away somewhere, then tugged at her arm. "I didn't plan on having company in the little hideaway the boys and I have been using, but I'm sure we can find something to do to pass the time."

Gabby shuddered when his touch softened to a rough caress, though the gesture seemed mechanical and somehow off. She dragged her feet a few steps, then intentionally bumped into a nearby pew. Drawing on a childhood spent as the consummate drama queen, she let a quaver enter her voice. "I…I can't see where I'm going."

"Bonus for me," Liam said, unperturbed. "I won't have to blindfold you." He dragged her another few steps before he growled a low oath and said, "You were walking just fine earlier. Either knock it off or I'll shoot your boyfriend."

Gabby forced a snort. "Not even close."

"Fine," Liam said. "I'll shoot you instead. But think about it. If I put a bullet in your foot or maybe a kneecap—you'll be tripping for real, and you wouldn't want that, would you? So I'd suggest you straighten up and start walking, Ms. Solaro."

Gabby gave in, walking meekly beside him. The moment they stepped outside Christ Church, thunder split the sky and the heavens opened in a torrent of rain, as though the very earth itself wanted to punish Liam for his sins.

Or maybe she was the one being punished. Again.

TY WAS DRENCHED within moments. His hair was slicked to his scalp and his clothing clung to his body, but he barely registered the discomfort as he doubled back around the church, his legs pumping and his pulse pounding in his veins.

He wasn't leaving without Gabby. The strategist in him still wasn't entirely sure she was innocent, but if she knew something about Liam or his plans, she was an asset. The law enforcement agent in him refused to allow an innocent—a female innocent at that—to be collateral damage if there was any way for him to prevent it. And the man in him—

He broke off the thought with a vicious curse. Moments later he rounded the corner of the building and saw two figures in the near distance, silhouetted in a flash of lightning. Then the darkness became an impenetrable wall of fog, and the drumming rain drowned out the sound of Liam's and Gabby's footsteps, leaving Ty effectively blind and deaf.

In a flash he was reminded of the text message he and each of his teammates had received moments before the blackout commenced: "Are you afraid of the dark?"

At the time he'd sneered, thinking it was a cruel joke from someone who knew him well enough to know that he didn't sleep, but not well enough to know why. Now he began to understand. Fear wasn't in the darkness.

It was in the isolation.

Focus, he told himself, trying to hear the words in his father's voice, reminding himself it wasn't just his life at stake or Gabby's. It was Grant Davis's life, and the lives of hundreds or even thousands of Bostonians, depending on the range of the device Liam had planted.

Telling himself he was focused, even though it was a lie, he ran toward the last place he'd seen them. Forget playing Liam's little game. He was going to grab the bastard here and now, and force him to divulge where Davis was being held.

Battle madness roared in Ty's head, tempered by the crisp, cool logic that'd been trained into him through years of experience. He skidded through a puddle, the noise splashing loud in his own ears, but hopefully deadened by the driving rain. He squinted through the fog but saw nothing. Unease took root at the thought that he'd lost them, that—

A car door opened nearby, bringing a glint of interior lighting. *There!* Ty thought, and bolted toward the vehicle. Through the mist, a car took shape. It was small and generic, and would have been completely unremarkable if Liam had gotten away and made it out of the city without being stopped at a roadblock.

Liam's mist-shadowed form bent over as he shoved Gabby through the driver's-side door and across. Before he could follow her into the vehicle, Ty slammed into the door, pinning Liam between the door and the frame.

He pushed down, hard, crushing the bastard in an unyielding metal grip.

Liam roared and shoved away from the car with almost superhuman strength. The door flew open, banging into Ty, who staggered back two steps, slipped on the wet pavement and fell. He caught a blur of movement in his peripheral vision and ducked, expecting a kick, then realized Liam wasn't focused on him. He was going back for Gabby.

"No!" With anger and desperation burning in his veins, Ty erupted from the pavement and lunged for Liam. He hauled the older man away from the car, dragged him across the sidewalk and slammed him up against the clapboard side of an historic house. "Leave her alone!"

He levered an arm across Liam's neck and pressed down until the bastard gurgled for breath. Then, nearly beyond himself, he yanked the weapon from Liam's underarm holster, cocked the revolver and pressed it to his temple.

"Don't move," he growled. "Don't even breathe."

Thunder boomed, underscoring his words, and the rain ran down Ty's body in rivulets, making him think of rain forest guerrilla warfare rather than urban streets. Faint light from a window above them illuminated the fog, giving him his first real look at Liam in a decade.

He'd shed the night-vision goggles he'd worn in the church, revealing lines of age and stress and anger fanning out from eyes Ty remembered as being bright green. The older man's hair was the same jet black it had been back then, but the easy smile of an officer born into wealth and rank had gone cold and mean, and when Ty looked into his eyes he didn't see a teammate looking back at him.

He saw a murderer. A sociopath.

Leaning in, he eased the pressure across Liam's throat so he could speak, then growled, "Where is Grant?"

The bastard should have been scared. Instead he smirked. "I told you. Follow the campaign trail, and stick with the proper order. You skip a step and he dies. That I promise you, and I remember you were always a stickler for promises."

"No games." Ty tapped Liam's temple with the barrel of his own gun. "Tell me where he is or you're dead, and your revenge dies with you."

Liam's eyes flashed in triumph. "That's where you're wrong. If you kill me, the bomb goes off at dawn and Davis will be blown to pieces." He paused, and that cold, cruel smile touched his lips again. "Besides, my revenge will live on in my sons."

"No, it won't." Ty watched carefully for the other man's reaction when he said, "Colin is in intensive care under police lockdown, Aidan is dead and Finn is in custody." He paused, registering Shea's blink of surprise that flattened to a cold mask. "They failed, Liam. You failed. It's over, so do yourself a favor and give it up. Nobody's listening to you, and you have nothing left to prove."

"I have *everything* to prove," Liam snarled, his face contorting with rage. "I spent ten years in prison because of Grant Davis. I lost my wife, my family, my future…everything."

"You were the one who disobeyed orders," Ty said, fury rising at the other man's intransigence. "Don't blame that on your teammates."

"Of course not," Liam sneered. "Especially not when I'm talking to a teammate who's always been blinded by hero worship." He paused, and something shifted in his eyes when he said, "We were friends once, and you were always smarter than the others. You saw things they didn't. That's why I saved you for last. But remember one thing… You bring in the authorities and Davis is dead. I'll be watching you."

He shifted lightning fast and yanked away from Ty, who lost his grip on Liam's rain-slicked clothes.

Roaring, Liam spun and jammed his foot into Ty's

gut, doubling him over, then stomped viciously behind his left knee. Fighting through the pain, Ty twisted, grabbed a fistful of Liam's coat and yanked. Unbalanced, Liam cursed and flailed his free arm, then wrenched free from the jacket and took off into the fog.

Ty took two steps after him, but his left leg gave way beneath him, sending him crashing to the pavement.

As he struggled back to his feet, a car door slammed and an engine revved. Then Liam took off with a squeal of tires, the headlights of the small car lighting the scene for a moment. Then the car disappeared into the fog, leaving Ty alone as the rain ended and the storm began to move away, grumbling to itself with fitful lightning flashes.

Ty hung his head and sucked in a breath. Then another. Then he quit breathing altogether when he suddenly remembered. "Gabby."

The word echoed along steamy streets that had gone quiet, save for the drip of water from eaves and parked cars. There was no response.

He couldn't believe he'd forgotten about her in the heat of battle, couldn't believe his responsibility to Grant Davis had completely blotted her from his thoughts for a brief period that could prove deadly.

Why can't you believe it? said a small voice inside him that sounded like Mandy's. *You've always put your country before everything else. Why should now be any different?*

And that stray thought was right. It shouldn't be any different. Grant was his protectee, his priority. Yet that didn't stop Ty's pulse from pounding in his veins, thundering in his head when he filled his lungs and shouted, "Gabby, damn it, answer me!"

Sudden moonlight poked through the rapidly clearing storm clouds. A dog barked in the distance, then another, closer by. Halfway up the street, a figure stepped out of the shadows.

"Ty?" Her voice held a faint tremor.

He crossed to her in five strides, grabbed her arms and held her away from him, just able to see her in the faint glint of moonlight. "You're okay?"

Her laugh was hollow, trailing off in a swallowed sob. "I'm not hurt, but I'm not okay, either. That man… He…" She pulled away from him and pressed the back of one trembling hand to her mouth. She took a deep breath before she said, "I escaped from the car when you grabbed him, but I didn't know where I was or where to hide. I thought…" This time when she trailed off, she shook her head and said simply, "I thought he was going to kill me."

Ty wanted to reassure her that he wouldn't have let that happen, but it would've been a lie. Once again he'd been too wrapped up in his own agenda to pay attention to others who needed his help.

Instead he said, "He's gone now. You're safe and—"

He broke off and muttered a low curse. "We're safe, but I don't know what comes next."

They stood there for a long moment, standing close enough that he could feel her warmth and smell her light, flowery scent on the humid air, close enough that he felt as though he should either step closer still or take a big step back.

Finally, she said, "What did he mean by 'follow the campaign trail'?"

"He was just talking," Ty said, frustration sharpening his tone. "If you've been on his Web site, you know Liam hates that Grant is the vice president and the heir apparent to the next round of nominations. It's ironic, really. We all thought Liam was the one who'd go on to be president someday."

"What if he wasn't just talking?" Gabby said. "He said something about an op being like a treasure hunt. What if it was a clue?" She paused. "Didn't President Stack make a swing through Boston during his last campaign?"

"No." Ty shook his head, but his pulse picked up a notch. "His plans changed at the last minute, so Grant took his place." *Follow the campaign trail.* "I was with him back then. He'd requested me for his protection detail."

He barely remembered the quick trip, just another one-dayer among many during those last few weeks before the election.

"Where did you go?" Gabby asked. When he didn't

answer right away, she pressed, "Ty, what was your first stop in Boston?"

"Let me check." He reached for his handheld, then cursed when he remembered that it was dead. Moments later the radio on his hip beeped. The long-range units had been handed out to the members of Davis's Secret Service detail who'd scattered to track down even the slimmest leads.

It was an alternative Ty knew he should consider. He could check in with his SAC and bring in the resources of the Secret Service and the other federal agencies. They'd have the itinerary from the Boston trip, along with the manpower to search each location. They had bomb dogs and additional agents en route, as every federal resource under the sun had converged on Boston.

But there was Liam, and as much as Ty wished he could discount the threats, he just couldn't.

When the radio beeped again, he pulled it out of his pocket. Instead of answering, he opened the back panel and shook out two rechargeable batteries, which he swapped into his flashlight. He clicked on the light and shone it on Gabby, who was pale and shaky but seemed otherwise okay. "Let there be light," he joked feebly, then winced when he remembered that the flashlight didn't matter to her.

He wasn't sure how he felt about her blindness, or the fact that she hadn't told him.

Then again, he wasn't exactly starting on the moral high ground when it came to full disclosure.

Her eyes were dark with fatigue and upset, and he could hear both in her voice when she said, "I want to go home."

"You can't," he said quietly, wishing he had a better answer for her. "Your place isn't safe, and I don't have time to get you to someone I trust. Besides, you know the city better than I do. I could use your help."

She tipped her head, and a sad smile ghosted across her lips. "And you're still not sure whether you're being set up. You want to believe me, but there's still the question of why Liam was in my apartment and how he knew my name. Until you figure it out, you're not letting me out of your sight."

"Something like that."

She looked at him for a long moment, her sightless eyes unerringly fixed on his face, before she nodded reluctant acceptance. "What's our first stop?"

Chapter Four

Dear Ty:

I missed you while you were away from your computer. I hope that doesn't set off your "needy alarm" or anything. I don't mean to cling or put a guilt trip on you like your ex used to. I just wanted you to know that I'm glad you're back online. Did you have a nice visit with your parents? I hope so; I envy you the relationship. I haven't spoken to my parents in...gosh, nearly a dozen years. Not that I blame them. I was a pretty unlikable kid. Some days I wish they could get to know me as an adult, though. And aren't I a total downer today? Chalk it up to the rain we're having here in Boston. I think I'll go hit my stash of Reese's Pieces and then go to bed before I piddle on anyone else's parade. I'll catch you later, and hey, welcome home!

[Sent by CyberGabby; May 3, 11:58:02]

12:50 a.m., August 3
4 Hours and 48 Minutes until Dawn

Ty breathed a sigh of relief when they reached the New England Aquarium, which had been the first stop on the Boston leg of the Stack/Grant campaign trail.

They'd walked, knowing a car would draw attention, given the curfew. Thankfully, they hadn't run into any cops or members of the Guard, and they'd managed to avoid the places where shouts, shots and the orange glow of fire warned that the looting had spread eastward.

A part of him—the part that had been dissatisfied by the routine of Secret Service work and had craved the excitement of Eclipse assignments—itched to dive into crowd control, but he had other priorities tonight.

At the thought of one of those priorities, he glanced over at Gabby. She had paused at the edge of the front court, and as he watched, her face relaxed into a smile. "We're here."

"How do you know?" he asked, struck by the subtle interplay of emotions.

"I can smell the salt water and chlorine." She gestured across the open court, to where a sheet of Plexiglas separated visitors from a pool of water and a rocky ledge beyond. "When I first moved to Boston, I used to come here and sit by the seals. I liked to listen to them bark at each other. They always sounded like they were talking to me."

Her words held a hint of loneliness, of secrets that almost had Ty asking more. Instead, he took her arm. "Come on. We need to search the area."

"What are we looking for?"

"I'll know it when I see it," he said shortly, then winced. "Sorry."

"Don't be. I'm blind. I deal."

"You sure do." Ty let his hand slide down her arm until their fingers linked and they were holding hands. On the walk over, he'd figured out that she did best if she had that contact, which allowed her to interpret shifts in his weight or pace and react accordingly.

He'd never been a touchy-feely sort of guy, even with Mandy, but this was expedience, nothing more.

Ignoring the faint buzz of disquiet brought on by the thought, he tugged her toward the ticket window. As they walked, he said, "Why a cane rather than a dog? I remember you saying you loved animals."

It was part idle curiosity and part a feeler designed to help him figure out how much of what she'd told him online was true. He knew he didn't have the right to ask for—or expect—that honesty, but that didn't stop him from wanting it.

"I'm on a waiting list," she answered after a moment. "Since I stay close to home, it isn't usually a problem." She reached out a hand and touched the rough stone facing of the ticket area, which was mocked up to look organic and rocky. "Do you see anything?"

He shook his head and cut the flashlight beam around, shining it into shadowy corners that yielded nothing but more shadows.

"There has to be something here," he said, frustrated. "A note or a clue or something. Otherwise why would Liam insist we come here?"

They quartered the open court at the front entrance, but found nothing. The aquarium itself was dark and locked tight, though a loud mechanical hum from behind the building suggested the personnel were running generators, no doubt fighting to keep the big tanks aerated and filtered.

Ty and Gabby worked their way around one side of the main building, where a series of loading docks provided access for the supplies needed to maintain both animals and tourists in grand style. Ty shone his light into each shadowed nook as Gabby followed behind him, the soft lines of her face set in concentration.

After a few minutes she said, "Why are we doing this? What does Liam want from us?"

"He's angry," Ty said shortly. "He wants revenge on the people he blames for his own mistakes." Then, realizing those were the obvious, unhelpful answers, he took a deep breath and tried to focus, tried to think rather than just react. "Eleven years ago, seven of us were recruited by Commander Tom Bradley for a rescue op in the Middle East. Fifty-eight civilians, including U.S. Secretary of State Geoffrey Rollins, were being held hostage in the middle of a civil war and it was our job to get them out. We each had our specialty—Liam was the electrical specialist, I was the demolitions man. I was supposed to set off a blast as a distraction, then he'd kill the power to the building where the hostages were being held. It was all split-second timing."

Ty paused, muscles tightening at the memory of the tense days and hours leading up to the rescue mission, then the moment it had all blown up in their faces. He continued, "Liam was angry even back then. Or maybe *entitled* is a better word. He'd grown up rich, and his father's money and political power had helped him get where he was going quicker than he would've otherwise. Our C.O. knew he was a loose cannon, knew he had a temper and hated the kidnappers. There'd been a car bombing a week or two earlier, and Liam was nearly killed, and a local woman died in his arms." He paused, knowing that war had marked each of them differently. "Anyway, whatever the reason, he rushed the job and cut the power before Tom signaled the attack. I hadn't set off the charge, the tangos weren't distracted, and they mounted a hell of a response, pinning us down while they set off cyanide gas grenades in the rooms where the hostages were being held."

Gabby sucked in a breath. "Oh, God."

They'd reached the place where the aquarium

building ended at the water and they could go no further without hitting Boston Harbor. Ty turned and headed them back the way they'd come, shining his light from side to side, but seeing the faces of the people they'd been sent to save over a decade earlier.

"We went in and took the bastards out," he said, his voice neutral from the hundreds of times he'd gone over the incident with his superiors, the thousands of times he'd replayed it in his own head. "We grabbed the hostages, gave them an antidote that helped fight the gas, got them out of their contaminated clothes. Most of them did okay. What we didn't know was that the secretary of state already had breathing problems. He didn't make it out." He took a deep breath and concluded with, "The aftermath was a political nightmare, though Washington kept as much of it out of the papers as possible. We all took a hit, but Liam took the fall. Not even his family's power could get him out of the court martial. He wound up doing ten years in a military prison."

Gabby was silent as they worked their way back to the main courtyard. "What does this have to do with the vice president?"

"Grant Davis was the team's tactical expert. Liam swears that Grant gave him the signal to cut the power, but he didn't." There was no question in Ty's mind. He knew the vice president too well to believe anything else. "And now Liam doesn't want revenge because

Grant did or didn't give the signal. He wants revenge because Grant has the life Liam thinks he should've had. He was the one who was supposed to go into politics, the one we all figured would be president someday." Ty paused. "Which brings us back to your question. What does Liam want? If he wanted me dead, he could've killed me back at your apartment, or at the church. But he didn't. He sent me on what's feeling a whole lot like a wild-goose chase.... But why?"

None of it made any sense, making Ty feel edgy and raw. He wanted to pull away from Gabby and pace the length of the pier, but that would burn energy he didn't have to waste, so he forced himself to stand still and think.

Still, the events refused to gel into anything approaching logic.

Gabby blew out a breath. "Maybe *why* doesn't matter right now. Maybe what matters is following his instructions while we try to figure out the rest. So let's find this clue he said would be here. He told you to follow the campaign trail, right? Where exactly did the vice president go when he was here? Did he visit the exhibits inside the aquarium?"

"No." Ty shook his head, trying to remember back to eighteen-plus months earlier. He would've given anything to switch the batteries back to his radio and call for the info, but he couldn't take the risk. *No authorities*, Liam had said. *I'll be watching.*

Ty hadn't seen him, but that didn't mean the bastard wasn't out there, doing exactly as he'd promised.

Knowing he couldn't take the risk of making contact, he forced himself to think, trying to pick out a single stop out of a blur of campaign travel and the chaos of planning and refining the candidate's protection at each stop.

"He didn't go inside," he said slowly, turning a wide circle and trying to imagine what the details around him would look like in daylight. "He gave a short speech…over there, I think." He pointed to the other side of the building.

Somehow following his gesture from the movement of his body, Gabby nodded. "Over by the harbor seal exhibit, you mean? Or behind it? There's a boat ramp, I think they use it for the stranding rescue boats."

"Yes, that's it!" He squeezed her hand, suddenly realizing that her local perspective could be more valuable than he'd thought. "The boat ramp." He tugged her in that direction, sure they were onto something. "It's coming back now. Grant gave his ecological conservation speech, touched on the fuel crisis and tied those issues back to the stranding rescue volunteers." He remembered how he and the other agents had vetoed Grant's grand plan of heading out into the harbor aboard the new rescue skiff he'd helped fund. "He christened their new boat the *Davis Discovery*. It was a damned good photo op, him standing next to the boat, smiling."

"Then that's where we need to look," Gabby said with quiet assurance. "Let's go."

"Watch the stairs. They're pretty slick."

They descended the short flight of stairs, which led to a cement ledge bounded by the rear of the harbor seal display on one side and the harbor on the other. A swing of the flashlight showed that there was a sturdy metal railing designed to keep the unwary from falling into the water, and a locked gate blocked off the end. Beyond it, a cement ledge descended into the water on a sloping angle. Three boats were tethered to the ramp and locked in place with chains. One looked vaguely familiar, but its name was the *Charter Bank Discovery,* suggesting it was mate to the boat Grant Davis had funded.

Ty looked around and saw nothing else but water, marble and cement. "Damn it. There's no message."

"There must be," Gabby insisted. "Where was Grant standing in the photo?"

"Down here." He tugged her to the end of the ramp, near where the boats were tethered. Feeling his brief burst of optimism draining away, he used his flashlight to search the shadows. As a last resort, he leaned partway through the railing and shone the light down near the waterline, where the harbor lapped against the cement boat ramp.

And saw it.

"Sonofabitch," he said quietly, when he saw the text chalked on the wall like graffiti, then louder, as his momentary excitement crashed to nothing. "Oh, hell."

The storm had washed away part of the message.

"WHAT DID YOU FIND?" Gabby asked quickly.

"A message. Or more precisely, part of a message." Frustration edged Ty's tone. "He wrote it at the waterline in some sort of water-soluble grease paint. The tide doesn't come up that far, but he must not have been expecting the storm. The rain washed off some of the writing. All I can make out is the letters *T* and *D*, then a gap, and the letter *T*, which doesn't help us one bit."

"Show me," Gabby said.

He hesitated for a moment, then took her hand. "You'll need to climb through the railing and lean way over. I won't let you fall."

"I know," she said, and let him guide her into position. It wasn't until she was nearly upside down, hanging over Boston Harbor anchored only by Ty's strong grip on the waistband of her shorts and his hand wrapped around one of her bare calves, that she realized she was putting more faith in Ty than she normally did in people she'd known for years. He'd lied to her and he'd dragged her into events that went far beyond her small sphere, yet she trusted him not to let her fall.

Then again, she supposed it made sense on some level. He wasn't the man he'd pretended to be during their late-night conversations. That man had been open and approachable, sharing her love of computers and community, along with the thirst for adventure she only let loose in her internet life. No, the real Ty Jones was hard and no-nonsense, and if he lived for adventure, it was the sort that came with guns and life-or-death politics, not bungee jumping and skydiving. Yet it was that very part of him that made her lean against his strong form and stretch her arm out to touch the water, then the rough cement surface above, trusting him.

He might be a liar, but he was also the sworn body-guard of one of the most powerful men in the country. He was, by his very nature, a protector.

He wouldn't let her fall.

"A little up and to your left," he said quietly.

She felt the faint change in texture, the smear of greasepaint on wet cement. "Got it." She traced the first two letters. "You're right, there's a *T* and a *D*, then nothing."

"Then we're at a dead end." He shifted and started to pull her up.

"Wait," she ordered. "I think I can get another letter or two." She traced her fingertips lightly along the wet cement, feeling where the rough texture went faintly slick. "I think there's a hyphen." Continuing on, she found an *S* and a *Y*. Then she shook her head. "There's probably one more letter before the T you found, but it's too far gone. You can pull me up now."

Once they were standing together on the boat ramp, she shook her head. "I'm sorry. TD-hyphen-SY-something-T sounds like gibberish to me."

Ty stiffened, his body going still and hard as granite. He muttered a low, vicious curse.

"What is it?"

"TD-SYDET," he said flatly. "Goddamn it. It's short for Time-Delay Sympathetic Detonator. He's telling me how to disarm the bomb he's hidden somewhere in the city. The one set to go off at dawn and take the vice president with it."

Automatically, Gabby's fingers went to her wrist, where her watch displayed the time in Braille. "It's just past one and the sun comes up around five-thirty. We've got four and a half hours. How many places did the vice president visit when he was in Boston?"

"Too many," Ty rasped. His fingers closed on her wrist. "Come on. We've got to haul ass."

Gabby resisted, pulling away and swinging to face him with her heart drumming in her ears and her throat nearly clogged with nerves. "You don't need me for this. In fact, the only thing I'm going to do is slow you down."

"I'm sure as hell not leaving you here."

"I know my way home." She forced bravado when her voice wanted to tremble. "I'll go to Maria's."

She didn't want to know about this, didn't want to

be part of it. All of a sudden, her online adventure had become far too real.

"Hiding out at a friend's house won't stop Liam from taking you," he said grimly. "Then you'd be endangering her, too." He tugged her to his side, still holding her hand as he had been since they left the church.

She resisted. "I don't… I'm not…" She blew out a breath and went with the truth, no matter how handicapped it made her look. "Despite what I told you about loving to travel, I've barely been anywhere besides the North End and the waterfront in years, Ty. I'm not comfortable in new places, and I'm not kidding when I say I'm going to slow you down the moment we step outside my comfort zone."

Instead of answering, he said, "You're doing fine so far."

"I get around okay with the cane, or someone leading me." She also felt less self-conscious at night, in the darkness, less like everyone nearby was watching her fumble, but he didn't need to know that. Nor did he need to know that her name had come up on the guide dog list twice now and she'd backed out, more than half-afraid that bad things would happen if she left her niche.

"I haven't been around many…what's the proper terminology these days? Sight-challenged people?"

"Blind people," she said. "Tell it like it is." She paused, then said, "I can see some light and dark when it's really bright out. It happened in an accident when I was fifteen, so I had the benefit of having sight half my life, and spending the other half learning to function without it."

She braced herself for the inevitable platitude, the pity. Instead he said, "You do it well."

"Not well enough," she said, feeling the familiar acid burn. "After I graduated from the Edmunds School, I lasted six months in the so-called real world before I came crawling back to the school, asking for a job."

"What happened?"

"Something that doesn't matter in the slightest right now," she said firmly. "The point is, you'll be far better off without me."

"No, I won't," he said simply, and tugged her along, not letting her resist this time. "Come on."

As she stumbled along beside him, not struggling nearly as hard as she knew she should, she wished she could see his face, wished she could tell what he was thinking.

Part of her wanted to wake up from this strange nightmare, where people carried guns and a time bomb was ticking down somewhere in the city. But part of her—that crazy, mixed-up part of her that had gotten her in so much trouble before—wanted to never wake up, wanted to keep living this adventure as long as she possibly could. Worse, there was a small, stupid corner of her soul that wanted to stay with him long enough to figure out how much of himself he'd put into those late-night e-mail exchanges.

She'd liked the person she'd gotten to know online. Maybe she could have loved him.

At the thought, she missed her footing and stumbled, slamming into Ty's solid body.

He caught her and held her against him, waiting for her to regain her footing. "You okay?"

No, she thought, *I'm an idiot who's managed to confuse fiction with reality.* But she wasn't quite brave enough to say such things aloud, not anymore. Besides, the feel of him against her, the press of his strong arms and the solidity of his body, which seemed cool in the hot, humid night, ignited feelings in her that jumbled the words in her brain and reminded her of just how long she'd been without a man, without a lover.

Reminded her that she'd dreamed of Ty in lurid Technicolor fantasies, and that she'd awakened wanting and alone.

"Sorry," she murmured, and levered herself away from him. "I told you I'd slow us down."

"It's okay." His voice had gone husky, sending a shimmer of awareness through her, a faint hope that the sudden flare of heat wasn't entirely one sided.

They stood there for a heartbeat in a sort of half embrace, arms wrapped around each other, bodies warming at the points of contact. Then, as one, they moved apart.

This was neither the time nor the place, Gabby knew, and even under the best of circumstances, what could possibly happen between them? He was a Secret Service agent. He guarded the vice president, for heaven's sake. The last thing a man like him needed was a woman like her.

She shrugged off the thought, shoving it deep down into the recesses of her mind as she said, "I guess you've got yourself a temporary partner, then. So, partner, want to tell me where we're going?"

"Boston Garden, or the Fleet Center, or the TD BankNorth Garden or whatever the hell they're calling it these days." He took her hand and their fingers twined together as he tugged her along. "Our second campaign stop was at a tutoring center right outside."

"That's halfway across the city!" Gabby fought to keep a tremor out of her voice. It'd been months since she'd been outside her familiar haunts, more than a year since the last time she'd left Boston.

"I stashed a car two blocks over. We'll have to risk the drive." Either he hadn't caught the tremor, or he was deliberately misunderstanding its cause. "Come on. There's a curb here, then stairs."

Gabby hesitated for a long moment, then took a deep breath and stepped out of her comfort zone.

MAYBE FIVE MINUTES LATER, as they skirted the wharf area just south of the aquarium, Gabby wrinkled her nose. "Smells like someone's catch went bad."

"And then some," Ty agreed, then cursed and dropped his voice to a near whisper. "Careful. There's someone up ahead of us."

"A cop or a looter?" Gabby hissed back.

"I'm not sure it matters at this point," Ty said quietly. "We have to avoid everyone. I can guarantee my boss went ballistic when I missed the last two meetings, and the radio gives off a homing signal, so he knows either I'm in trouble or I pulled the batteries and went off the grid. I'm betting there's a BOLO out for me at this point, and we can't afford to be seen. It'd take too long to talk our way out of a stop, and we don't know how or how often Liam is keeping tabs on us. If he sees us talking to someone, anyone, he could panic. I won't let that happen."

Gabby's stomach knotted. "What are we going to do?"

"We'll skirt the back side of the processing shed and work our way around this guy. With a little bit of luck we'll be past him and at the car in five."

He transferred her hand to his belt, leaving his hands free as he moved out with her in tow. They moved swiftly but silently, and Gabby was grateful for the flat rubber soles of her sandals.

Adrenaline buzzed through her system as she followed him, straining her acute hearing in an effort to track where they were, and where the other man might be. Inwardly, she chanted, *Please be a cop, please be a cop,* because no matter what Ty said, she'd rather meet up with a cop than a looter. Last night Maria's brother had brought rumors of the terrible things that were happening just a few miles away. "They're tearing open the stores and stealing stuff," he'd said. "Busting up parked cars, fighting each other for the loot, setting things on fire. It's a real mess." His voice had dropped before he'd added, "There've been some shootings, too. Rapes. It's getting ugly down there."

Now, feeling her legs start to shake, Gabby put her head down and prayed, *Please let him be a cop. Please let us get by safely.*

As Ty changed direction, looping around the back side of the pier, she heard water lapping down and to her left, and felt sound vibrations bounce off a long wall to her right. The strong, fishy smell identified it as the sorting shed the fishermen used to divide their catch.

The surface underfoot felt and sounded like a mix of slick wood and rough concrete, and Gabby didn't want to think about what might be in the puddles that wet her toes. She and Ty finished their three-sided circuit of the sorting shed and turned south once again on what she was pretty sure was Atlantic Avenue, the main road paralleling the harbor. Once they were back on the sidewalk, Ty whispered, "We're past him. Let's move out."

He lengthened his strides until they were moving fast, almost running the final half block to his car.

Gabby was breathing hard by the time he skidded to a stop. Ty caught her hand from his belt and guided her touch to the vehicle. "This is it."

The waxed metal felt smooth and almost alien beneath her fingertips. "Yours?"

"Nah." There was faint derision in his voice. "Standard issue federal field office sedan I borrowed from the scene. I prefer classics for personal use."

"I remember," she said faintly, feeling an unexpected jolt when the small piece of their online charade clicked with reality.

"You?"

"I used to like hot rods." She swallowed back a bubble of nausea. "I mostly walk these days. I get a little carsick now." Make that viciously, violently carsick from a combination of vertigo and posttraumatic stress.

She heard the beep and click of power locks disengaging, and reached for the door handle, telling herself she could do this. She took a deep breath and opened the door, just as footsteps sounded behind her and a man's voice said, "I need you to step away from the car, Jones. The boss is looking for you."

Ty cursed, and metal rasped on leather as he drew down on what could only be a fellow officer. "Stay where you are, Ledbetter." Gabby heard the pitch of his voice change when he turned toward her. "Get in the car."

"But, Ty, what if—"

"Get in the car. Now."

The measured urgency of his tone, the almost dead calm, had her body obeying even before her mind caught up with the situation.

She dropped into the car and shut the door, but he must've had the driver's door open, because she could clearly hear the other man say, "Don't make this tougher than it needs to be, Ty. You're off the grid, and that doesn't look good. You and I both know you didn't have a damn thing to do with Patriot's disappearance, but the boss can't take any chances. Even worse, the locals sent out a BOLO for you before we could. Seems like a woman went missing after she met up with you. Her apartment's trashed and there was signs of a struggle." The other agent's voice changed as he shifted position and called, "Miss Solaro? Are you okay?"

"She's fine," Ty said before she could answer. "And I need you to stand down and walk away. If you don't, I'm going to have to do something neither of us will enjoy."

"Come on, Ty, let's be—"

A sharp crack of gunfire cut him off. Moments later Ty was in the car and they were peeling away from the scene.

Gabby didn't ask. All she could do was clamp her arms across her midsection and double over as fear pressed in around her and tears and nausea competed to overwhelm her. "Pull over when you can," she said miserably. "I'm going to be sick."

Chapter Five

Dear Ty:
It's no real secret, and you shouldn't feel strange asking. My parents kicked me out when I was sixteen. Sure, they called it "going away to school in Boston," but we all knew I wasn't supposed to come back when I graduated. I snuck out of the house one too many times, raced one too many street rods, got hauled to the MDPD one too many times. It was for the best, really. Getting kicked out was a serious wakeup call, and I don't know where I would've ended up if it hadn't happened. One of these days I should call and tell them I'm grateful, and that I ended up okay after all. [Sent by CyberGabby; May 30, 5:15:52 a.m.]

1:32 a.m., August 3
4 Hours and 6 Minutes until Dawn

Ty muttered, "Come on, come on," as he drove, sending the car hurtling through the city, dodging wrecked and abandoned vehicles, using the sidewalks when the roads were blocked. He knew they'd have to ditch the vehicle soon, before they wound up helicopter bait, but he wanted to put as much distance as possible between them and the wounded agent, Ledbetter, before he stopped again.

Firing on Ledbetter had made things a hundred times worse than they'd been before, but he hadn't had any other choice.

He couldn't afford to be brought in. Not now. Not before dawn.

"You didn't actually shoot him, right?"

He glanced over at Gabby, who'd gone very pale in the aftermath of a quick, vicious bout of nausea. She clutched the door handle with a white-knuckled grip, and shuddered when he cornered too fast.

He fought back an uncharacteristic urge to soothe. "I got close enough to send him for cover," he said gruffly. Then, knowing there was no real value in adding another lie to the tally, he exhaled and said, "I winged him. That was the only way to be sure Liam would believe I wasn't talking to the feds." He paused. "Hang on. Wicked turn coming up."

They screamed around a corner almost on two wheels as he went one street over in an effort to avoid Faneuil Hall, which glowed orange with the efforts of the looters.

The back end of the vehicle cut loose in the second

half of the turn. Ty swore and wrestled the car back under control, skin prickling with adrenaline at the close call.

He was driving with no headlights in an effort to avoid detection until the last possible moment. Unfortunately, that also meant he could barely see the damn road in the moonlight.

Gabby murmured something that sounded like a prayer. He half expected her to order him to pull over at the next police station and let her out. Hell, he wouldn't have blamed her. He might've even done it, and taken his chances with Liam. But instead she said, "The agent said something about Patriot. Was that the vice president's code name?"

"It *is* his code name." Ty refused to even consider the possibility that Grant might already be dead.

"Did you give it to him?"

"How'd you know?"

"Lucky guess, based on some of the stuff you wrote me about your boss." She paused. "Why Patriot?"

"Because that's exactly what he is. He's…" He trailed off, looking for the words, wanting her to understand how important Grant Davis was, not just to him, but to the presidency. The country. Distilling it down, he said, "I met him for the first time right before the hostage rescue op in the Middle East. Him and Liam both. The two men couldn't have been more different—Liam was a smart rich man's son who knew exactly where he was going in politics and how he was going to get there, while Grant was middle-class America all the way. He'd started at the bottom of the enlisted ranks and scratched his way up from there. He didn't have the same book smarts as Liam, but he had street smarts, and he did what needed doing, exactly when it mattered most. Commander Bradley put him in charge of tactics, and he put together a hell of a plan. Would've worked, too, if it hadn't been for Liam getting an itchy trigger finger."

He paused, remembering, and wanting her to understand. "After it went wrong, we got the hostages out, and we knew the insurgents had wired the building to blow. When Commander Bradley took a head count and we realized Liam wasn't with us, Grant didn't even hesitate. He went back in." He glanced over and found her focused on him rather than the pitch of the vehicle as he swung around a corner. He continued, "It was like something out of the movies. The building was going up all around them, flames everywhere, shrapnel flying, smoke and dust so thick you could barely see through it…then Grant comes out, carrying Liam on his back." He paused. "That's what makes him a hero."

"And a patriot?"

"Everything he's done since then makes him a patriot," Ty insisted. "He's worked his ass off to protect the environment, improve working conditions, build outreach networks and improve education, first as a senator, and now in the White House. Some people might see the vice presidency as a figurehead position full of photo ops, but Grant is living proof that the position can be as much as the occupant chooses to make it."

Realizing he'd started to sound like one of Grant's campaign speeches, Ty winced and fell silent.

After a moment, Gabby said "He's lucky to have a friend like you."

"Would've been luckier if I'd been on my toes at the Hancock Building." The failure still rankled. If he'd been a fraction quicker in his response, a heartbeat faster to figure out what was going on, he might've been able to grab Liam before things spiraled so far out of control.

He hadn't been fast enough, though, and the failure cut deep, as did the fear that he wouldn't be fast enough this time, either. Worse, he was beginning to realize his priorities had shifted when he wasn't looking. Now he wasn't just concerned about finding Grant and defusing the bomb. Somewhere along the line, Gabby had become part of the equation, too. He had to keep her safe, had to help her do the things she couldn't on her own. He'd taken her out of her element, and now she was depending on him, which was exactly the sort of situation he'd tried to avoid with every woman who'd passed through his life since Mandy.

Don't depend on me, he wanted to say. *I'm only going to let you down in the end.*

"You're staring at me," she said suddenly, turning her pale, luminous eyes toward him. "I can feel it. What's wrong?"

Nothing, he thought. *Except I'm beginning to wish I really was just a normal single guy who e-mailed you out of the blue through Webmatch.*

"We're close enough," he said abruptly, aiming the car toward for the mouth of a deserted parking garage. "We'll ditch the car inside before Ledbetter puts the word out and they retask a chopper to find us."

She nodded, but her porcelain skin went a shade paler, and he saw her swallow hard. "Whatever you think's best. I'm out of my element here."

The question was, why did she hide herself away? She wasn't shy and retiring, either online or in person, and she seemed to be able to get around just fine with a cane or a guide. So why was she hiding out in the North End and surfing the net for companionship?

Ty almost asked, almost referred back to the things she'd told him on all those late nights, when the dreams had woken him, he'd gone looking for someone to talk to and found her awake as well. But he didn't ask, because he knew that he damn well couldn't go back and undo the lies he'd told her, and he couldn't go forward, either. *They* couldn't go forward, no matter how strong the attraction. There was no future in it, and another lie wouldn't be fair to either of them.

So instead of asking, he parked the car just inside the main entrance of the covered garage, turned it off and pocketed the keys. "Come on. We'll be on foot from here."

"Can't say I'm sad to hear that." Gabby climbed out and stood, pressing a hand to her stomach. "At this point, though I'm not sure if I'm still nauseated or if my body thinks it's time for breakfast."

At the reminder, Ty glanced at his watch. They had four hours until dawn, give or take, and three more campaign stops that he could remember.

"We'll have to make it fast, but I've got some rations in here." He popped the trunk and dug through the ready kit he'd dumped in the car out of habit. The rucksack was packed both for emergencies and for Eclipse deployments, which could come at any time, funneled to them via Dana Whitley, the supersmart Pentagon staffer who formed their only link to the U.S. Government.

At the thought of Dana, Ty paused as the glimmer of an idea came to him.

It might even work.

First things first, though. He pawed through his ready kit and pulled out a half-dozen chocolate protein bars, the candy bars that were both his guilty pleasure and a damned good source of quick energy, and a six-pack of bottled water. He tucked the provisions in a smaller knapsack and added a med kit containing first-aid supplies along with some odds and ends. "Here." He passed Gabby a candy bar and bottle of water and took a bottle for himself. "It's either a midnight snack or a really early breakfast."

He collected his spare ammo clips from a light-weight lockbox, loaded them into a utility belt and strapped the belt around his hips. Then he slung the knapsack over his shoulder and slammed the trunk.

He was weighted down now, and less mobile than ideal, but he had to take what he thought they might need, because they wouldn't be coming back for the vehicle.

Hell, for all he knew, Ledbetter had planted a bug on the thing the moment he found it.

"I can carry something," Gabby offered around a mouthful of chocolate.

"I've got it," Ty said. "But I could use your help. I need you to stand watch while I make a call. You'll hear a car or helicopter a lot sooner than I'd see it."

She nodded and held out a hand for him to lead her into position. When he turned away, though, she caught his arm. "Who are you calling?"

"A friend." She knew that his three former team-mates had already been the targets of Liam's wrath, but she didn't know that the four of them still worked together, risking their lives on a regular basis. The existence of Eclipse was on a need-to-know basis, and he didn't figure she needed to know.

Like Mandy didn't need to know? a sly voice asked from deep inside him, where the guilt lived. He ignored the question, knowing he'd hear it again as soon as he slept.

"Just signal if you hear anything, okay?" He left her near the doorway, trusting her to guard his back, and plugged his cell charger into the car's power port. When he got enough juice to brighten the computerized display, he typed in a quick text message to Dana. She was in Washington, true, and couldn't help him much from there, but if Shane, Chase or Ethan managed to get through to a working phone, they'd call her first. It was his best shot at getting a message through.

The cell signal was seriously weak, though. Either the parking garage was blocking it, or the cells themselves had finally gone down due to lack of power.

Ty cursed when the message failed three times in a row. He was on his fourth try when Gabby called, "You'd better hurry. Something's coming. A helicopter, I think."

"On my way." Ty yanked the cord free and pocketed it along with the phone. He hoped like hell it found a cell and sent his message before the battery used up the meager charge he'd been able to put in it.

Fingers crossed on that one.

He shouldered the knapsack and jogged to the parking garage entrance. He paused and listened, and could just make out the noise of an incoming chopper over the sounds of fighting a few streets over. "The looters are on the move."

"I know. I can hear them." Gabby's expression tightened. "Tell me we're going the other way."

"I won't let anything happen to you," he said, and took her hand.

They both knew that wasn't the answer she'd been looking for. More important, they both knew he hadn't promised to keep her safe. He'd told her more than once that he never made a promise he couldn't keep, and he knew from experience that it wasn't always possible to keep another person safe, no matter how much he might want to.

Sometimes bad things just happened.

GABBY TRIED TO MOVE and breathe as quietly as she possibly could as Ty led her past North Station, which was just opposite the Garden. The noises coming from a few streets over made it seem like a war zone, with shouts and screams, the clanking sounds of heavy machinery and the occasional chatter of gunfire.

"This way," Ty murmured, tugging her down what felt and sounded like a narrow alley between two tall buildings. Picturing it, and picturing what would happen if the authorities blocked one end and the looters blocked the other, Gabby shivered and moved closer to his reassuringly solid bulk. He squeezed her fingers. "Almost there."

Moments later they hung a left and the echoes fell away on Gabby's right, telling her that they were back on a main road. The air smelled of stale grease and spices from vendors' carts, along with the tang of spoilage where food had gone to waste in the power outage. More, the heavy dampness in the air warned her that it was nighttime but beginning to edge toward dawn.

"Here." Ty stopped. "This is where Grant gave his speech. They built the speaker's platform here and ran power from the learning center."

"What's wrong?" Gabby asked, picking up on a new thread of tension in his body, in his voice.

"The learning center's closed."

"Of course it is. It's like one in the morning in the middle of a blackout." She paused. "We could break in. It's not as if we don't already have the cops after us." And how many years had it been since she'd said something like that? Twelve years, she knew. Twelve years since she'd traded the streets for darkness, since she'd given up adventure for safety, and she was just now coming to realize how much she'd missed the adrenaline rush.

It couldn't last beyond tonight, she knew. Even if she and Ty came out alive past the dawn, it would still be over. He would return to his world and she to hers. But for now, she thought on a strange, misplaced burst of excitement, for tonight, she got to live again.

There shouldn't have been joy amidst the danger,

but for Gabby, there was a moment of sight. Of beauty. Of wishing for things she couldn't have, ever again.

Things like her vision. An adventure.

A man like Tyler Jones.

"It's not a question of breaking in," he said. "The learning center isn't here anymore. It's shut down. The place is a coffee shop now."

"You're sure we're in the right spot?"

"Positive." He tugged her forward. "Here's Liam's message, loud and clear, scrawled on the coffee shop door with a black marker. It says 'C-4' followed by the number sign and '50'. Then 'propane x 2.' He's telling me how much of what explosive he's used."

Hearing Ty's voice go hollow, Gabby asked, "What sort of a blast radius are we talking about?"

He was silent for a moment before he said, "A device like that could take out anywhere from a single building to a city block, depending on its placement, shielding and a couple of other variables. And what do you know about blast radii?"

"I listen to the TV while I work on the computer. I'm blind, not cloistered." When she realized that had come out more sharply than she'd intended, she blew out a breath. "Sorry. I guess I'm not as calm about all this as I thought I was."

He squeezed her hand. "You're doing great." He stood there another long moment, then turned away as the rotor sounds swung nearer. "Come on, we've got what we came for. Our next stop is only a few blocks away, maybe a mile tops. I'd take the car, but that chopper's too damn close already. Do you think you can make it on foot?"

Gabby hadn't been tired before then, but the moment he asked the question, she felt the burning in her calves and the dry dust of sleeplessness behind her eyeballs. It was late, she'd already walked farther than she usually did in a week, and she was far from home.

Suddenly she felt weak and vulnerable, and frighteningly out of place.

Her bravado of a few minutes earlier drained away, warning her that she'd been kidding herself. This wasn't an adventure at all. It was real life, and it was real danger. But it was life-and-death danger and not just for her. If that bomb went off at dawn, people were going to die. That meant she didn't have the option of being tired right now.

So she nodded. "I can make it. You got any more of that chocolate? I could use a sugar buzz."

He chuckled low in his chest, the vibration running through her where their bodies pressed together, making her realize they were standing closer than she'd realized. "That's my girl," he said.

She felt him shift, felt him turn to face her and lean in, but she wasn't prepared at all for what he did next.

He leaned in and kissed her.

TY MEANT THE GESTURE as a thank-you for her support, for her bravery, hell, for not losing it and breaking down in a quivering mass of tears, which was what he figured plenty of women in her position would've done.

At least, he told himself that was the intention. But the moment his lips touched hers, he realized the gut-punch truth. It was far more complicated than that…and far simpler.

He was attracted to her. The moment she'd stepped out of the shadows in that North End courtyard, he'd felt a click of connection, a flare of heat that was nearly as foreign to him as the openness of their e-mail exchanges had been.

And in that moment, he'd fallen a little bit in lust with the woman who'd accidentally become his friend.

He'd lied about his job and the real reason he'd contacted her in the first place, but over the months that followed, the things he'd told her had been real. He'd shown her pieces of himself that hadn't seen the light for years, perhaps since even before Mandy, and there was nothing simple about that.

There was also nothing simple about kissing her, but the moment his lips touched hers, the moment he swallowed her startled gasp, he realized he didn't give a damn about the complications.

She was sweet and soft in the darkness, a welcome respite from the nightmares. When her lips parted hesitantly beneath his, he deepened the kiss and touched his tongue to hers.

Power rose up inside him. Heat. Needs he'd thought burned out of him long ago swept through his body, reminding him of things he'd gone far too long without.

She moaned at the back of her throat, a sexy purr that nearly blasted him through the stratosphere on a surge of lust. Of want. Of need. Of—

Oh, hell, what was he doing?

Ty jerked away from her, breathing hard, aroused and ashamed at the same time. His heart hammered against his ribs as he stared at her in the moonlight, at the moist fullness of her lips and the way her full breasts rose and fell beneath her pink button-down shirt. He wanted to take her in his arms and kiss her again, to sink into the sweetness until everything else went away.

Instead, feeling like a jerk, he released her and stepped back. "I'm sorry. I shouldn't have done that."

She almost hid the flinch, but he'd grown attuned to her movements and expressions over the past few hours, and he caught the faint wince, which made him feel even worse.

He reached for her hand. "Gabby, listen, I—"

"Don't," she said, interrupting him. "Please don't. I understand."

When she pressed her lips together and looked

away, he said, "I don't think you do understand. It has nothing to do with you. It's me."

"Let's just forget about it." She smiled at him, the expression almost reaching her eyes. "It's not like it was a big deal. It was just a kiss after all, right?"

"Right," he said automatically, hating the pressure in his chest that said it might've been more than that for him, complications and all.

"You said we were hoofing it?" she asked, forcing him back on a track he never should've left in the first place. "Where to?"

He turned away, then reached back for her hand. "The Wellbrook Halfway House. It's at the edge of South Boston."

She faltered. "Southie? Isn't that where the worst of the looting is going on?"

"Yeah." He locked his jaw, knowing that this was where things were going to start getting ugly. "Stay close. We're headed into the war zone."

THEY WALKED in silence, partly to avoid detection and partly because there didn't seem to be much to say.

Gabby was proud of how she'd handled herself in the wake of that unexpected kiss. Then again, it wasn't as if he was the first guy to give her the old standby line. *It's not you, it's me.* That's what they said when they really meant, *It's you, but I don't want to hurt your feelings, so I'll pretend it's my fault even though we both know the truth.*

Her lips felt tender from Ty's kiss, which had been rough and tender at the same time, and pretty much everything she'd imagined it might be, plus interest.

Arousal still buzzed beneath her skin, but her heart ached faintly from the letdown. She told herself to take the kiss for what it was—an exciting moment amidst too many others in a single night. But that rang false even to her.

The whole situation wasn't an adventure; it was a disaster in the making. A runaway freight train of incidents that'd landed her on the run with a sexy agent who'd kissed her and pulled away, who'd shared himself with her only to reveal that he'd lied.

I want to go home, Gabby thought out of nowhere. She felt tears burn her eyes, matching in intensity the ache in her calves and feet. There was a dry rasp at the back of her throat. She told herself it was from thirst, not the sobs she held in her cheek.

"Here." Ty unslung his knapsack and pressed two protein bars into her free hand. "Eat these and chase them with some water. You'll feel better."

She wanted to snap that she was fine, but they both knew she wasn't, so she scowled and unwrapped the first bar as they walked.

She bit in and made a face. "You eat these things on purpose?"

"They may taste like salted cardboard, but they do the trick. You need to stop for a minute and rest your feet? Now would be a good time if you do. From here on in, we'll be on high alert."

She shook her head. "Let's keep going." *Let's get this over with.*

It took them a solid thirty minutes to reach the halfway house, though thankfully they managed to avoid both the looters and the cops. Still, by the time Ty led her up a set of stairs, she was tired and edgy and tense.

Ty sounded equally frustrated when he snapped, "What the hell is going on here?"

"What's wrong?" she said. "Don't tell me this place has gone out of business, too?"

"No, but something's not right. The Wellbrook Halfway House is supposed to be subsidized up the wazoo, but it looks like hell. The building's practically falling apart."

"Do you see Liam's message?"

"Not right off the bat. Stay here for a second. I'm going to take a look." He left her on the porch but returned in under a minute. "Nothing. Something tells me what we're looking for isn't written on the wall this time. I have a strong suspicion it's inside the house, not outside. Problem is, that means we've got to get inside, and we're not exactly within visiting hours right now."

He knocked sharply on the door. When there was no answer, he knocked again, raised his voice and called, "Hello? Is anyone in there?"

After a third round of pounding and shouts, footsteps sounded inside and paused, then the door opened partway and stopped on the jangle of a safety chain.

A man's voice, deep and gruff with age, said, "For chrissakes, it's nearly 2:00 a.m. Keep your voice down or you'll wake the kids."

"I'm sorry," Ty said. "I wouldn't have knocked, but this is quite literally a matter of life or death." Then he paused, and Gabby could all but hear him wrestle with the decision of how much to reveal, how much to keep hidden. Finally he said, "My name is Ty Jones. By any chance did an older, dark-haired man leave something here for me—a message, maybe, or a package?"

"Hold on." The door rattled shut, and the man called out something in an undertone, the words lost through the thick panel. There was a feminine query and a mumbled response. Then the door cracked open and a woman's voice said, "What did you say your name was again?"

"Ty Jones, ma'am."

"Are you with the Secret Service?"

Ty stiffened and Gabby felt a jolt of adrenaline at the hope that maybe, possibly, some of their questions could be answered.

"Yes, ma'am," Ty said carefully. "How did you know that?"

The security chain rattled and the door swung inward. "I think you'd better come in."

Chapter Six

Dear Gabby:
Sorry I haven't been around much lately, sweetheart. Work has been…well, it's been work. Lots of travel, lots of meetings, not a ton of downtime for email. My protectee is a good guy, though. He's really trustworthy and good about noticing the people who work for him. That, and the things he's able to get done…they make the hours worthwhile. I wouldn't change it for the world.
[Sent by TyJ; June 6, 12:00:05 p.m.]

2:01 a.m., August 3
3 Hours and 37 Minutes until Dawn

If Ty could've left Gabby outside where there was room to run, he would have done just that, but although they'd managed to avoid the looters on their way in, there was no guarantee that a knot of skirmishers wouldn't turn their way at any moment. Besides,

where could she run to? Without her cane or the famil-
iarity of known streets, she was at least partly depen-
dent on him for direction.

All of that meant she wasn't any safer outside alone
than she was inside with him, but the responsibility
weighed heavily as he stepped through the door of the
Wellbrook Halfway House and the man shut and
locked it at their backs.

Ty's flashlight beam showed the man to be in his
midfifties, with a thick layer of laborer's muscle
beneath a white T-shirt and worn jeans. The woman
hovering just behind him was thin and wore a striped
track-type suit that was trendy in cut, chain-store in
quality. She was probably a good ten years younger
than the man, but they wore matching wedding bands
and identical gaunt, tired expressions.

"This way," she said, gesturing for them to follow
her down a narrow corridor, which Ty's flashlight
showed to have yellowed wallpaper on the walls and
thin carpeting on the floor. She touched a finger to her
lips. "Quietly, if you don't mind. Most of the residents
sleep lightly, if at all, and we're having even more
trouble than usual with the little ones because there's
no electricity to run the fans."

Ty urged Gabby ahead of him, wanting to keep his
body between her and the older man, just in case things
went south.

It didn't feel like a trap to him, but he couldn't have

said exactly *what* it felt like. He was adrift without his usual teammates, without contact of any kind. Worse, the evidence he was seeing with his own two eyes was starting to add up and tell him impossible things.

When they reached the kitchen, the woman clicked on a battery-powered camping lantern. The light brightened the room, serving only to underscore the general shabbiness of the place.

The kitchen was restaurant-sized, and clearly set up to feed a hoard, with a huge stove, two refrigerators and a chest freezer tucked under the long vinyl-covered counter that wrapped around three sides of the room. A conference room table took up one end of the space, surrounded by enough chairs to seat fifteen or twenty people. The appliances were relatively new, and the glass-fronted overhead cupboards showcased a wide range of pots, pans and plates, but a wide crack marred one of the glass panels, and several of the cupboards were empty.

The overall impression was one of a once-successful operation running on a shoestring budget that only covered a fraction of the operating costs.

The woman gestured for them to sit. "Take a load off."

Ty remained standing. "You have a message for me?"

Her eyes crinkled at the corners. "He said you were the impatient sort. He also said it was important for you to see, not just hear."

"See what?"

"Sit down before your lady friend falls down," the man grumbled from behind him. "She's as white as a ghost."

It wasn't fatigue that had her so pale, Ty knew. It was nerves, if not outright fear. Knowing it, he took her hand and led her to one of the chairs. "Go ahead," he murmured. "Remember, I'm not going to let anything happen to you."

There it was again, that not-quite promise he couldn't be sure of keeping, no matter how good his intentions or how hard he tried.

When he took the chair beside her, he kept hold of her hand. Looking from the man to the woman and back again, he said, "Who are you and what am I supposed to see?"

The need to hurry burned in his blood. Alongside that imperative lurked a twist of disquiet, though he couldn't yet say why.

"I'm Leonore Wellbrook," the woman said. "Lennie." She waved to the man. "My husband, Tom. We run this place. As far as what you're supposed to see, James didn't say, exactly. We sort of figured you'd know."

"James?"

Tom frowned. "James Sullivan, of course. Don't you know him? Didn't he send you? Isn't that why you're here at this godawful hour in the middle of a blackout?"

Lennie patted her husband on the arm. "Of course he knows James, dear." She smiled beatifically at Ty.

"He's our angel. We wouldn't still be here if it weren't for him. He's kept us going this past year."

Ty felt like he was lost at sea. Sullivan was the name of Liam's ex-wife, the name his sons had taken after the divorce. It stood to reason that this "James" was an assumed name taken by one of the sons, or more likely by Liam himself. But none of the rest of it made sense.

If there was a pattern here, he wasn't seeing it. Or more accurately, he didn't *want* to see it, he acknowledged inwardly.

Look at this, Liam seemed to be saying. *Look at what's become of your hero's campaign promises.*

"I was in the area a couple of years ago," Ty said slowly, feeling his way. "This place looked like it was doing fine back then."

"We were," Tom agreed. "Two years ago, we upgraded the kitchen and the bedrooms on a federal grant. We even ordered a new heating system and all new pipes because they assured us there'd be another twenty thousand coming. All we had to do was apply for it, they said." He took his wife's hand. "We got our pictures in the paper shaking hands with the muckety-mucks. They took a few shots with some of the kids we had staying here, and then boom, they were out of town on their little feel-good campaign trail. The next thing we knew, there were bills due and the grant money up and disappeared on us, thanks to Grant Davis pulling the plug on the program."

His wife took over the story on a heavy sigh. "We've been trying to catch up ever since. Lord knows, we would've been foreclosed on six months ago if it weren't for James. He's sent us enough to let us keep our doors open. Like I said before, he's our angel."

"James isn't who you think he is." A cool wash of anger chilled in Ty's blood. "There must've been some sort of glitch in the paperwork. I'm on Vice President Grant's protection detail, and I know him pretty well. He'd never renege on a promise, and he sure as hell wouldn't leave a place like this high and dry."

"Then begging your pardon, *he's* not who *you* think he is." Tom rose to his feet and pulled a flashlight out of his back pocket. "Come on, I'll show you."

Torn between needing to know and wanting to get them both the hell out of there, Ty stood and pulled Gabby to her feet beside him. "You can show both of us."

Lennie stood. "Actually, I'd like a moment with Gabby. Please."

Ty hesitated. Logically, he knew these people weren't on his side. They were Liam's friends, and somehow Grant Davis's enemies. But they also appeared to be the glue holding the Wellbrook Halfway House together, and he saw a dignified plea in the woman's clear, tired eyes. Not deception. Not a threat.

He turned to Gabby. "What do you think?"

"I'll go with her," she said without missing a beat, and squeezed his fingers. "I'll be okay."

He nodded, knowing she'd pick up on the gesture even though she couldn't see it. Wishing he could give her one of his weapons, just in case, but knowing he couldn't, he let go of her hand. "Yell if you need me."

"We'll be fine."

Then she was gone, with Leonore leading her out of the kitchen through a second darkened hallway. The camping lantern cast a globe of light that flared and then died with the distance. Their footsteps creaked on the stairs, and a child's fitful cry from the second floor suggested Tom had been right when he'd said the occupants of the halfway house didn't sleep soundly.

The women's footsteps turned a corner, and Ty heard a door shut quietly upstairs. When there were no shouts or sounds of a struggle, he let out the breath he wasn't even aware he'd been holding, and turned to the older man. "What did you want to show me?"

Tom turned away and gestured with his flashlight. "This way. And brace yourself. I have a feeling you're not going to like it."

UPSTAIRS, LENNIE GUIDED Gabby into a small room that smelled of crowding and sleep, with an overtone of cheap air freshener. A bedroom.

"We'd normally have three or four kids staying in here together, or a family," Lennie said, her voice low in deference to the others Gabby could sense on the second floor. "But we lost some to the mob."

Gabby winced. "They were hurt?"

"They took off and joined 'em." The older woman shut the door to the bedroom with more force than necessary. "Which means they won't be welcome back here when they're done. Blackout or no blackout, Tom and I have our standards and we'll stick by them."

"You two are doing a good thing here," Gabby said, still feeling her way in the situation. She got a good vibe off Lennie and her husband, and Ty must have felt the same or he would've insisted they stay together. But assuming that this James person was actually Liam Shea, where did that leave them? What was Shea trying to prove through the Wellbrook Halfway House?

"This is Kayleigh," Lennie said, breaking into Gabby's thoughts. "Kayleigh, honey, say hello to Miss Gabby."

"Why?" The word came in the sulky tones of a preteen girl, one who'd been sitting alone in the darkness and didn't want anyone to know she cared.

"I think you two will be able to figure that one out for yourselves," Lennie said cryptically. Then, before Gabby could protest, she'd turned and left the room, shutting the door in her wake.

Silence echoed in the room, a tense, resentful quiet broken only when the girl said, "What are you, some kind of social worker? And why the hell are you here so late?" A glimmer of hope entered her tone. "Did you find my grandma after all?"

Gabby's heart broke on the question. She knew how it felt to have a family finally give up. But she also knew what pity felt like, so she said only, "I'm a computer teacher. As for why I'm here so late, that's a really long story." She paused, not sure where to go from here. "Lennie must be proud of you for not going with the others."

Sullenness flashed to outright anger in a second. "Is that supposed to be some sort of a joke?"

"No," Gabby said simply, sensing too much of herself in the girl to take offense. "Why would it be?"

"What are you," Kayleigh snapped, "blind or something?"

"As a matter of fact, I am. That means you're going to have to explain it to me." Gabby paused, then asked again, "Why'd they leave you behind?"

There was a long silence. Then, a quiet answer. "Because I've got a wicked limp and they say I slow them down."

"Oh." Gabby winced to hear the echo of her words to Ty earlier that night. *I'll slow you down,* she'd said, when she'd really meant that even if he told himself he didn't mind that she was different, it would grow old eventually. He'd think of how much easier it would be if she could see and do all the things other women could see and do, how much more of an asset she could be to the case, to his career, to his—

Stop it, she told herself fiercely. *Ty isn't Jeffrey. The situations aren't the same.*

For one, she and Ty weren't in a relationship; maybe part of her had wanted to imagine that online chitchat and e-dates counted as a relationship of sorts, but she'd never expected it to progress beyond that, had never planned to meet him in person. Now that she had, it was even clearer that nothing could happen between them. If her blindness would've been a liability in Jeffrey's world—at least according to Jeff—she knew for real that it would be far worse in Ty's.

In Jeff's world of corporate up-and-comers, being blind meant she used the wrong fork sometimes, or fumbled ungracefully when important people were watching. In Ty's world, it could mean the edge between life and death.

The thought, which came out of nowhere, brought an involuntary shiver. Part fear, part temptation, it shimmered in her belly like prescience.

"I wasn't always like this, you know," Kayleigh said. From her tone Gabby knew she was trying to prove how much she didn't care what the grown-ups thought of her, even though she so clearly did care. "It happened when I was nine. I was fooling around with my brother, Ben, out on the fire escape. Mama told us to knock it off and come inside, but we started wrestling instead, and I fell…" She trailed off, but Gabby could fill in the rest, partly from her own experiences, partly from knowing what sort of things could land a child in the custody of protective services.

Her heart ached for the girl, but she knew Leonore hadn't brought her up here to pity the child, so she took a deep breath and said, "You wanted to know how come I'm here so late? I came here with a Secret Service agent. We're looking for the man who's responsible for the blackout."

She didn't know whether it was supposed to be a secret that the blackout wasn't due to power plant overload in the wake of the recent heat wave, but she figured it couldn't hurt to tell this one child…and it might even help.

As she'd half expected, Kayleigh scoffed. "Yeah, right. A spy working with a—with someone like you. I don't think so."

"Not a spy," Gabby corrected. "A Secret Service agent. They're more like bodyguards than spies. Very, very smart bodyguards." Bodyguards who liked classic cars and rock and roll, and talked to her in the dead of night when the rest of the world was asleep.

"Still…how come he's working with you instead of someone else?"

Circumstances, Gabby thought, but aloud she said, "Because I know things he doesn't. I know this city pretty well, and I can move around in the darkness better than most people. Some of what you need light to see, I can tell from echoes of sound, or from the smell, or vibrations in the air…" She shrugged. "Sometimes I'm not even sure how I can tell something, only that I can."

When she said it like that, she realized being blind didn't sound like such a handicap. Then again, she was telling the kid what she needed to hear, that being different wasn't the end of all the fun stuff.

Only some of it.

"Well, that's kinda cool," the girl admitted. "But I don't have any spidey senses. I've got a crooked leg and a cane that makes my arm hurt when I use it. Ain't no spies going to come looking for my help." She paused, and Gabby wished she could see the girl's face when she continued. Her voice was so soft it was nearly inaudible. "There ain't nobody going to come looking for me."

Although Gabby couldn't see Kayleigh's expression, the wistfulness came through loud and clear, even through the remaining ring of teenage attitude. *They didn't want me,* it said. *They left me behind and went on with their lives, and I don't know how to catch up.*

Because she knew how that felt, because she knew how much that hurt, Gabby decided to do something she hadn't done in a long, long time.

She took a deep breath and started the story where it began. "When I was your age, I could see just fine…."

TY'S HEAD HURT by the time he left the small room that
served as Tom's office for the business end of running
the Wellbrook Halfway House.

The painful pressure drummed in his sinuses and
behind his eyeballs, and it wasn't just the product of
low blood sugar and nearly forty hours without sleep.
It also came from confusion. Denial. The battle between what he knew in his heart and what he'd just
been shown.

As he climbed to the second floor, using his flashlight to light the way up the creaking stairs, he tried to
figure out what was real and what was the trick. He
knew there had to be a trick. It was the only logical explanation for the letters Tom had shown him.

He just wasn't sure anymore who was the tricker
and who was the trickee in this scenario, and he was
looking forward to discussing it with Gabby on the
way to their next stop.

The very thought had him hesitating midstep.

Since when did he talk things out? He'd never been
much of a joiner, preferring to keep his own counsel
and gather all the evidence before passing judgment.
On the protection details, he was part of the team, yet
also a man apart. He didn't hang out with the other
agents, didn't do the beer-and-ballgame routine. That
was partly because his freelancing assignments with
Eclipse took up a good chunk of his spare time, and
partly because he didn't really need anyone else. He

was fine by himself. At least he had been, until he met Gabby online.

Their e-mail exchanges had made the nights seem shorter, the nightmares ever so slightly more bearable, and that only added to the problems he'd brought roaring to the forefront by kissing her when he should have stayed the hell away.

The worst part was, having kissed her once, he was itching to do it again, to do more, to explore the sort of chemistry he'd never expected, the kind of attraction he hadn't been braced for.

"Focus," he muttered to himself, and crossed the short distance from the stairs to the doorway Tom had indicated. Gabby was inside, talking to a girl.

The door was thin, and made of a wooden shell over a hollow interior, which explained why he could hear the voices quite clearly.

But there was no real explanation for why he didn't knock or twist the doorknob and let himself inside.

Instead he clicked off the flashlight, and listened.

"I grew up near Miami, and I pretty much did whatever I wanted from the age of twelve," he heard Gabby say. "I smoked, drank, raced cars, stole, fooled around with guys who were way too old for me. You name it, I tried it at least once, usually twice, to make sure I wasn't mistaken the first time." Her voice sounded different than usual, with an added vibrancy that suggested that no matter what had come of those years, not all of the memories were bad ones.

The revelation wasn't that much of a surprise. Over the past few months, and more strongly in the past few hours, he'd begun to suspect that Gabby had hidden layers, hidden histories.

He pressed closer, straining to hear as a second, younger voice said, "Your parents took off, too, huh?"

"No, they were right there in Miami, still married and doing the best they could to raise me and my sister, Amy." Gabby paused. "I guess I was an exception to the rule that dysfunctional families make dysfunctional kids. I was a juvenile delinquent who grew up with two parents, a sister, a dog and a nice house. I just….I don't know. I wanted to live every second of my life. I wanted to see it all, to do it all, to try everything right away."

"There's nothing wrong with that," the child said, her voice suddenly sounding far older than it had before.

"Yes, there is," Gabby contradicted quietly. "It was selfish and self-destructive, and I…well, I got what was coming to me sooner than even my father predicted during the worst of his famous 'why can't you be more like your sister' lectures."

This time when she paused, Ty imagined her taking a deep breath, pictured her looking somewhere inside herself, her luminous brown eyes focusing inward. The mental picture was so clear he thought he could've reached out and touched her, except they were separated by the door and he was listening in on a conversation he had no part of.

This is what it must be like for her, he thought. *A soundtrack with no picture. Voices only, leaving the rest to the imagination.*

Which made him wonder how she pictured him, what she thought of him.

And whether he had any right to ask.

"What happened?" It was the girl's voice, but it might as well have been Ty asking the question. Even though he could guess at least part of the story based on hints and conjecture, he found himself pressing closer to the door, needing to hear it in her own words.

"I was fifteen. I was with this boy." Gabby laughed, but the false sound couldn't hide the crack of pain in her voice. "Isn't that how these stories always start? Anyway, we were racing his souped-up old Camaro against some rich kid's daddy's Jaguar. He missed a turn and the Camaro skidded into a parking lot, hit a minivan and flipped end-over-end."

When she paused, the kid prompted her with, "You hurt your eyes?"

"Yes, though I didn't know it then. At the time, we both walked away from the crash, and lucky for us, nobody was in the parking lot when we hit. We didn't kill ourselves or anyone else, though the Camaro and the minivan were total losses."

She broke off, and Ty sensed that she was skimming over stuff she didn't want the kid to know. Important stuff. Stuff that made her voice go rough when she said, "A few weeks later I started having trouble with my eyes. Things were going all blurry. I couldn't see stuff on the board at school, I couldn't read very well…and it just kept getting worse. Problem was, I'd pulled the 'poor me' routine just about every other time I'd gotten in real trouble, and my parents were sick of it. The more they told me to get over it, the madder I got, until I just stopped talking about it. By the time they figured out something really *was* wrong with my eyes and took me to a doctor, it was too late for the doctors to reverse the damage to the optic nerve. The ocular surgeons went in and corrected the problem so it wouldn't get any worse, but they said I'd never get back the sight I'd lost."

"Did you?"

"Nope. I was legally blind before I hit my sweet sixteen, moved away from home a month after my birthday and haven't been back since."

"Your parents kicked you out for going blind? That really stinks." The kid sounded more resigned than outraged, reminding Ty that he'd been damn lucky in the family department, and he owed his parents a phone call when all this was over.

The thought of the future—and the present—had Ty clicking on the flashlight and reaching for the doorknob. But before he got the door open, Gabby said, "They didn't kick me out, I went. It was easier for all of us. Besides, I—" She broke off and turned when Ty entered the room.

"Who're you?" the kid demanded. She was maybe thirteen, crinkle-haired and old-eyed, with a blanket thrown over her legs even though the air in the small room was still and uncomfortably warm.

Before he could answer, Gabby's features softened, then clouded again. "Ty. How long have you been there?"

"Not long." He didn't elaborate because he didn't want to lie to her any more than he wanted to admit he'd been eavesdropping.

In the glow of the flashlight, he noticed how her pink button-down shirt clung to her curves in the humidity, outlining the generous swells of her breasts and giving a glimpse of cleavage. He noted, too, how the yellow light cast her skin in warm, golden tones and glinted on her chestnut hair.

As many times as he told himself to stop noticing the body of a woman he didn't plan to pursue, he couldn't seem to kill the awareness or the low throb of need.

Instead of dealing with any of that, he went with the practicalities of the situation, and their deadline. "I'm sorry, Gabby. We need to go."

Gabby glanced toward Kayleigh. "Can I have one more minute?"

"Sure, but make it quick. I'll be outside when you're

ready." Ty left the room and shut the door behind him, his thoughts a messy jumble of lust and reality. This time he crossed the hallway and leaned on the wall and told himself not to listen.

That didn't stop him from wondering, though, and imagining what it could be like to kiss her with no reservations between them, no danger and no ticking clock—just a man and a woman together because they wanted to be.

Chapter Seven

TyJ: Are you awake, sweetheart?

CyberGabby: I'm here. Can't sleep?

TyJ: Funky dreams. What's your excuse?

CyberGabby: Remember that idea I was telling you about for 3-D Web imaging? I started putting together a prototype the other day and it's really coming along. I can't seem to put it down long enough to go to bed.

TyJ: I can guarantee you wouldn't have that problem if I were there...

CyberGabby: Hah. Big talker when there's no chance in hell of that happening. You want to tell me about the dream?

TyJ: I'd rather talk about your prototype. Or you could tell me what you're wearing.

CyberGabby: Naughty boy...

[Instant message initiated June 6, 3:08:28 a.m.]

2:35 a.m., August 3
3 Hours and 3 Minutes until Dawn

"That the spy?" Kayleigh challenged once Ty was gone and the door had shut behind him.

"I told you, he's a Secret Service agent, not a spy. But yes, that's him." Gabby nearly sagged back against the bedroom wall, wishing she were as cool as her voice had sounded.

How much had Ty overheard? She had to assume he'd heard all of it—and she hated that he'd heard it that way. She would've told him the story if he'd asked. Instead, he'd gotten the watered-down, G-rated version.

Maybe that was best, she thought on a faint slide of disappointment. He'd already known that she was estranged from her family. Now he knew why, more or less.

"He's superhot," the child observed, her voice sounding too old, too worldly for a kid her age.

Gabby knew she and Ty were on a deadline, but she couldn't stop herself from saying, "Describe him to me."

There was a stunned pause. "Holy crap, you can't see him. You're running around with a guy who looks like he should be in the movies, and you don't even know it."

"Never mind, I shouldn't have asked. Besides, we have to go." Gabby stood, swiping suddenly damp palms on her wrinkled shorts. "I just wanted another minute alone with you so I could be sure you got what I was saying earlier. I didn't tell you about what happened to me to scare you or make you feel bad for me. I wanted you to know…life changes when something like that happens, but it doesn't mean it's over. When I moved here, I went to a wonderful school and met people like me. They taught us to mainstream, to function in the sighted world. They taught us to be stronger rather than weaker."

Gabby paused, realizing that she was the fatal flaw in her own argument. She'd managed less than six months in the real world before she got her heart broken and, perhaps more important, her ego badly dented, and she'd gone into full retreat mode. So much for stronger rather than weaker.

"Ain't no school for lame-os," Kayleigh said, picking up on another flaw. "And even if there was, I couldn't pay for it. There's just regular school, where they make fun of me, and the streets, where they take off on me." She lowered her voice and muttered, "Just like my ma did."

Gabby's heart ached for the child, and she wished she knew what Lennie had hoped to accomplish by putting them together. As far as she could tell, she'd just made things worse, dangling a solution and then snatching it away. *Oops, sorry, kid. That won't work for you.*

"I'll help you," she said impulsively. "I'll come back and we'll do some research. If there's one thing I know how to do better than most people, it's find stuff on the Internet. If there's a doctor who can help your leg, or a program that'll get you into a better school, we'll find it and we'll get you where you need to be."

Kayleigh hesitated a moment, then sighed. "We don't have a computer here."

"I'll take care of it." But Gabby heard the girl's real argument. *You're just saying all that. You won't really come back.* Because she remembered what despair felt like, she said, "Do you have something around here to write with?"

"I guess." Kayleigh's response might've been sullen, but moments later Gabby heard a rustle of bed-clothes and the shuffling sound of someone feeling around in the darkness. "Yeah."

Gabby gave the girl her phone number and e-mail address. "If you don't have a computer here, maybe they have one at your school or the library you could use. Or you can call me. I mean it."

And she did, she realized, even if it meant taking the Orange Line all the way out to Southie and using her cane to tap her way through the rough neighbor-hood in order to make good on the promise.

The idea was frightening. It was also tempting, an opportunity to help someone who needed her more than the nucleus of students and friends she'd gathered around herself like a shield.

When Ty cleared his throat out in the hall, she

stood. "I'm sorry. We have to go now, but I promise I'll be back."

And, like Ty, Gabby didn't make promises she couldn't keep.

She'd crossed the tiny room and had her hand on the doorknob when Kayleigh said softly, "Are you really helping him find a bad guy?"

There was a wistful quality to the question, one that found an echo deep inside Gabby and had her smiling ever so slightly. "Yeah." She nodded, more to affirm it to herself than anything. "I really am."

Ty GOT THEM OUT of the Wellbrook Halfway House as fast as he could, with only a nod to Tom and Lennie. "I'll be in touch."

He could tell from their expressions that they wouldn't be holding their breath until his return.

Then again, if what Tom had shown him was the truth, then he didn't blame them for their lack of faith. If the letters were real, and not part of some elaborate mind game perpetrated by Liam and staged by the residents of the Wellbrook Halfway House, then they had every right to their suspicions, because they'd been promised the moon and been handed a lump of garbage.

Beside him on the sidewalk outside the halfway house, Gabby shivered faintly. "It's cooled off."

"Here." Ty shrugged out of his windbreaker and draped it over her shoulders.

"What about you?"

"I'm fine." In fact, it was probably better this way, because the jacket had covered his holsters. In this neighborhood, particularly in these circumstances, he'd feel better having his weapons in plain view and easy access. Call it an implied threat. *You don't bother me, I won't put a hole in you.*

When she'd finished donning his jacket and rolling up the sleeves, he took her hand. "Come on. Our last stop, unless Liam changes the rules on us, is an admin building at Boston General Hospital." He paused and took a breath. "I'm sorry, Gabby. We still can't risk a vehicle. We're going to have to hoof it."

"Let's go, then." She followed his lead out to the street without protest, and his respect for her, which was already far too high for his comfort, edged up another notch.

Most of the women he'd met, including the trained field agents, would've been close to the end of their reserves at this point. Gabby, though, soldiered on and did what needed doing. He wanted to tell her he was proud of her, that she blew him away.

Instead he tightened his grip on her hand and led her into the night. As he walked, he thought about what Tom had shown him, about what it might mean.

They traveled several blocks in a silence broken by shouts, sirens and helicopter rotor thumps off to the south. Thankfully, it sounded as though the riots were beginning to either die down or move farther away.

The churn inside Ty's head, however, continued unabated, souring his mood and making him feel restless and a little mean. He wanted to hit something, to fight someone. He wanted to drive fast, to blow something up, to make love to a willing woman.

To make love to Gabby.

"Back there, Tom showed me some letters," he said abruptly. "Official forms from something called the Urban Improvement Fund. Some were from before the campaign trip, promising him a three-tiered grant spread out over two years, partly for improvements to the building, partly for education and remedial programs. There was even supposed to be money for a counselor." He wasn't familiar with the actual programs, but the paperwork had sure as hell looked legit. "The newspapers went to town on it, talking about how the work would help revitalize the neighborhood and help transition singles and families from the streets back onto the grid."

When he fell silent, Gabby glanced over at him. "What happened? Did the funding get cut?"

"I'm not sure it ever existed." That would be the first thing he'd check. "Once the election was over and President Stack and Vice President Davis were inaugurated, he and Lennie got a couple of letters about senate budget cuts and alternate funding sources, and then one final form letter announcing the dissolution of the Urban Improvement Fund." He paused, acid churning in his gut. "By that time they'd committed to the improvements they'd outlined in their grant proposal. They've had to cut corners almost everywhere else in order to pay off the work. Meanwhile, other parts of the house and the program are falling apart."

Tom had openly admitted that, hindsight being twenty-twenty, they never should've contracted for work without having the money in hand. They'd gotten caught up in grand plans, and he swore they'd been egged on by their contact at the Urban Improvement Fund, who'd disappeared right around the same time the grant went kaput.

"That's terrible, and of course I feel for them." Gabby said quietly, "But budget cuts happen, and sometimes worthy causes suffer. I don't see the connection to what's happening here."

"According to Tom, Grant Davis was deeply involved in the Urban Improvement Fund. That's why he stopped at the halfway house during his campaign swing, and why he made a special point to schedule all the photo ops. The project was supposedly his baby."

"That should be easy enough to check."

"If we had power and computer access, sure," Ty said sourly. "Unfortunately, we don't have either between now and dawn, so we can't check anything.

Which, no doubt, was part of Liam's plan—to cut me off from my resources and then twist things around until I can't figure out which way is up anymore."

They walked half a block in silence before Gabby said, "Did Liam leave you a message about the bomb?"

"No." And that worried the hell out of him. Had he missed a clue, or was there something else going on?

Gabby furrowed her brow in concentration. "Liam couldn't have known about me, or if he knew you had a fake online girlfriend in Boston, there's no way he could've predicted you'd drag me along with you. So that thankfully rules out little Kayleigh being involved. Which means he wanted you to know about the Urban Improvement Fund."

"I'm with you there." Ty tugged on her hand, guiding her to his side so her body bumped against his at hip and shoulder. "Pothole," he said, by way of explanation, and wondered if he was trying to explain it to himself or her.

The cool night crowded him. He'd killed the flashlight to avoid attracting attention, and the moonlight cast deep shadows on either side of them. Feeling the prickle at his nape that warned they were being watched from one of the row houses they'd passed, he moved closer to Gabby and adjusted his automatic in its holster, just in case.

Or maybe there was nobody watching, and the sense of unease came from within.

Gabby seemed to sense his tension. Her voice bordered on tentative when she said, "I know you said the vice president is a good man, but what if—"

"Stop," he said harshly, interrupting before she could voice the suspicion Liam was trying to plant in his head. "It wasn't Grant. If anything, someone close to him is trying to make him look bad. Maybe even Liam himself."

The Gabby he'd first met face-to-face, the one who'd switched places with a friend and hidden in the shadows, would have let it go. The Gabby who'd escaped from Liam in the church and run from the cops an hour later, the one who'd bared her soul in an effort to help a child…that Gabby lifted her chin and said, "Don't talk over me just because you don't like what I'm saying. Is that how the Secret Service investigates threats to their protectees? By ignoring the interpretations they don't like?"

"Of course not, but—"

"But nothing," she said, interrupting him this time. "Take your own emotions out of the equation for a minute and pretend Grant Davis isn't your friend. What do you see?"

"I see that Liam Shea is a very smart man who is looking for revenge and is perfectly willing to kill to get what he wants. Given that, it's no leap to believe he'd manipulate evidence in order to take down the most powerful of the men he blames for how his life turned out." Ty clenched his free hand into a fist, almost wishing one of the nearby shadows would turn out to be a threat, and give him a target for his frustration. "It's really almost simple. It's not enough for Liam to simply kill Grant. He's determined to destroy his reputation, too. He wants to kill the Patriot's legacy."

"What about you?" Gabby asked softly. "Why hasn't Liam attacked you directly? You were one of those men. You were there when the rescue went wrong. For all we know, he blames you for not setting off the diversion in time. So why hasn't he tried to kill you?"

"Because he knows he's already taken away the most important thing— The man I've sworn to protect with my life."

It wasn't until Ty said the words aloud that he realized how sad that sounded. Liam had hurt Chase and Ethan by targeting their families, and he'd gotten to Shane by hitting at the company he'd sweated blood to bring to the top of the security world. Ty didn't have a family of his own, didn't have a company of his own. He had his relationship with Grant, which was part friendship, part hero worship.

At what point had that become enough for him?

Shaken by the errant thought, Ty continued, "By taking Grant on my watch, Liam struck at both of us. Now he's getting off on seeing me flail around as I try to make it through his stupid treasure hunt before the bomb goes off."

"What if it's more than a scavenger hunt?" Gabby said, her expression pensive in the moonlight. "What if he's trying to tell you something?"

"Then I'm not listening," Ty said shortly. "And this conversation is pointless."

He expected her to snap back at him or lapse into silence. Instead she said softly, "The idea wouldn't make you angry if part of you didn't think there was something to it." She paused, waiting for a response. When he marched along, his jaw clenched, she said, "You can see the pattern. The boat at the aquarium wasn't named after the vice president any more. The tutoring center is closed. The halfway house—"

"Stop!" he said sharply. "Just stop, okay? You don't know anything about what's going on here. You don't know Liam or Grant, or what either of them is capable of, and I don't need you playing amateur sleuth or trying to crawl inside my head. The only reason you're here is because I don't know where Liam is or when he's watching, and I'll be damned if I let another—" He clicked his teeth together on an oath, on the anger he knew wasn't really directed at her, and fought to gain some semblance of calm. When he thought the words would come out sounding a shade more reasonable, he said, "Look, I don't mean to be a complete jerk, but just back off a little, okay? I'm not used to working with anyone else, and you're crowding me."

"Well, excuse me," she said, her fingers going stiff in his. "I don't remember asking you to come see me while you were in town. In fact, I'm pretty sure I said to stay away."

"Until you talked Maria into pretending to be you, of course." Realizing he was close to shouting, Ty reined himself in with a mental yank and cursed under his breath. "Listen, Gabby, I didn't mean to—"

He broke off when he caught a flicker of motion out of his peripheral vision. At the second flicker, he transferred Gabby's grip to his belt and hissed, "Stay behind me. We've got company."

A low chuckle emerged from the shadows between two row houses, followed by the silhouette of a man, or rather a boy in his late teens, slim-hipped beneath low-hanging jeans, wearing an unbuttoned Red Sox jersey and a matching cap turned sideways. He seemed to glide across the pavement, sinuous and snakelike, an impression that was reinforced by the smoothness of his chest and his shaved-bald scalp beneath the ball cap.

"Company," he said, his voice soft and almost sweet. "Doesn't that sound all friendly and stuff? Since we're being friendly, I'll introduce myself. I'm Snake, and these here are my boys."

Footsteps shuffled as other teens emerged from the

shadows all around Ty and Gabby, ringing them, hemming them in. There were ten in all, each one bigger than the last, until the final figure stepped up, a mammoth young man, maybe nineteen or twenty, with huge biceps and no neck.

Ty palmed the flashlight and flicked it on, shining it directly in No-Neck's eyes for the distraction factor. "We're not looking for trouble here, guys."

A quick scan told him they didn't have any guns he could see, but they were holding enough pipes and knives to do some serious damage.

Snake bared his teeth, showing off a pair of filed-sharp canines. "Maybe we are." His eyes fixed on Ty's semi-automatic, then slid to Gabby. "You think you can take all of us before we take her, tough guy?"

Ty cursed inwardly when Snake's eyes flicked to his hardware. Odds were that they wanted his guns more than they wanted Gabby, but he wasn't willing to play those odds any more than he intended to surrender his weapons to a street gang.

Problem was, he couldn't very well distract them while Gabby took off on her own without guidance, which left him pretty thin on options.

"Think about it, guys. You don't want to do this," he said quietly.

Snake's teeth flashed again. "Why not?"

Because I'm a federal agent, you moron, Ty thought, but didn't say because it would probably make things worse. Instead, he flicked his light around the circle. Based on their hesitation and the lack of visible gang colors or tats, he was willing to bet they were an offshoot of the riots, not an organized street gang. Even better, he caught a couple of nervous shuffles when he moved the flashlight beam from face to face.

If there was a weak spot in the circle, he should be able to exploit it. "This blackout isn't going to last forever," he said, locking eyes with one of the shufflers. "When it's over, the cops are going to come looking for the punks who had their fun tonight. You sure you want to be those guys?"

The shuffler wavered, broke eye contact and began to edge away. Victory flared in Ty's veins and he eased back, using his body to herd Gabby toward the weak spot in the human circle, hoping she'd understand.

Get ready to run, he thought, wishing she could read his mind. *That way.*

"Yeah." Snake swaggered forward with No-Neck at his side. "As a matter of fact, I *do* want to be one of those guys. Starting now." He gestured to Ty's underarm holster. "Hand it over, butt first, and no funny stuff or we'll make the lady suffer."

"Okay, okay." Ty held his hands out, indicating no harm, no foul. He reached into his holster, moving slowly, and came up with the 9mm, holding it by the butt with two fingers. "Let's not do anything we'll all regret."

He flipped the weapon, caught it by the grip and shot Snake.

The punk shouted and went down, clutching his upper arm. In the stunned moment before all hell broke loose, Ty killed the flashlight and grabbed Gabby's hand. "Run!"

He lunged through the gap the shuffler had left in the circle. The kid went down with a grunt, and Ty staggered free, dragging Gabby after him, as a roar went up from the gang.

"Get him!" No-Neck's bellow was nearly lost under a high-pitched wail from Snake, but it did the trick.

The punks spun and charged.

He knew he couldn't shoot all of them, not in the dark, running, with only fifteen in the mag and one spare clip, along with the slower revolver. Instead Ty opted for full-out retreat.

He and Gabby raced along the street. He led her along the road itself, not trusting the shadows because violence had a nasty habit of attracting more of itself from the darkness. Though the moonlight made it easier for him to run flat-out with Gabby in tow, it made things equally easy for their pursuers, who were younger and faster.

Hopped up on rage and adrenaline and whatever else they'd been into that night, the street toughs howled threats and imprecations as they closed in fast.

"We've got to get off the street," Gabby said urgently. "Do you see anywhere to hide?"

"It's all houses, and they're locked up tight."

"We're right near the edge of Southie, right? I think there are shops up one street and over." She gestured north.

"It's better than nothing. Come on!" Ty spun, raised his weapon and sent two shots over the punks' heads, close enough to scatter them. Then he turned down the next cross street and put on the afterburners.

He and Gabby ran across one block and up the next. His legs burned and his lungs ached, and he could only imagine how she was feeling by now.

When she stumbled, he steadied her and risked a look behind them.

Pursuit was half a block back and gaining.

"Come on, sweetheart, only a little farther," he urged, the endearment slipping out before he could call it back, before he could flash on how right it felt to say it aloud after having typed it so many times.

"I can't," she cried, her steps faltering and slowing. Her lungs heaved in great gasps and he could feel her trembling. She'd finally reached the end of her reserves, and he couldn't blame her.

He also couldn't let her stop.

Hoping to buy them a little more time, he turned and fired off three more shots. Their pursuers scattered again, only this time not all of them made it. One of the punks took a bullet and went down, sprawled in the street as he writhed in pain. Ty felt a flash of remorse, but he couldn't let it slow him down.

"Lean on me." He didn't give her a chance to protest, just looped an arm around her waist and supported most of her weight as they ran on into the darkness. Another fifty yards and they reached a cross street, where he saw the edge of the commercial district diagonally across from them.

Along with the signs of vicious looting.

The few windows not covered by security gratings or metal pull-down accordions were smashed in, the storefront contents either taken or broken and scattered across the sidewalk. Small fires still smoldered in places, leaving the air thick with smoke.

"Are they gone?" Gabby said, her voice thin through her labored breathing.

"The main action is gone, but those other guys are right behind us." Ty surveyed his limited options and picked the nearest potential hiding spot. "This way. Hurry."

They raced across the intersection and he boosted her through a broken storefront window, then followed close behind. There was no alarm, no emergency lights, suggesting that the backup batteries had died sometime during the blackout.

"Chocolate," Gabby said quietly. "I smell chocolate and…cigarette smoke."

Ty sniffed and found the air thick with the heavy scents. "It's a candy store. I don't know about the cigarettes. The looters, probably." He urged her down from the front display. "Come on. We need to get out of sight."

Debris crunched underfoot, making the going slippery and uncertain.

He didn't dare use the flashlight, knowing it'd shine beacon-bright in comparison to the rest of the storefronts, so he tried to feel his way deeper into the shop with Gabby in tow. He made it maybe six steps before his foot knocked against a solid object and something fell with a loud crash.

"Damn it." He froze, listening for a response. When there were no shouts, no sounds of approaching footfalls, he blew out a breath. "We got lucky that time. I wouldn't count on it happening again."

"Let me lead."

Ty stifled his immediate protest, seeing the logic. She'd spent almost half her life feeling her way around in the darkness.

He took her hand, not as her guide this time, but as her follower. "I'm all yours."

He hadn't meant the double entendre, but he didn't call it back, either, and a strange sort of intimacy draped itself around them as he followed her lead.

The air grew thick as they worked their way past upended display tables, stepping on candy the looters had smashed underfoot. Moonlight filtered in through the broken window, providing some light, but Ty forced himself to let Gabby choose her course. Then, once they turned a corner and followed what felt like a short hallway, the light cut out, leaving him completely in the dark.

Liam's gibe ghosted through his brain. *Are you afraid of the dark?*

As he followed Gabby's tugging hand and whispered directions, trying not to crash into anything else, part of Ty gained new appreciation for what she must go through on a daily basis. Another part of him wished like hell he could turn on the flashlight. Sensitivity to the physically challenged was one thing. A federal agent without light or night vision was another. He felt toothless and vulnerable, and hated both.

She led him through the retail shop to a series of back rooms, and then guided his fingertips to a metal door that was locked on the inside.

"Emergency exit?" she whispered.

"I think so. Nice job," he whispered, and felt her breath feather on his face, warning him that they were too close for comfort.

Ty stepped back and reached down to unlock the dead bolt. He turned the handle slowly, then eased the door open a crack and paused.

The sounds of active fighting came through all too loud and clear. Bullhorn-amplified official orders to cease and desist were nearly drowned out beneath the roar of a mob and the sounds of shouts and shots. Flames licked the windows of a cement-faced building not fifty yards away, and a man charged past, screaming victory and holding a shotgun over his head. He was silhouetted black against the orange light for half a second and then was gone.

Keeping a death grip on the doorknob and angling his body to resist if anyone tried to yank the door open, Ty eased the panel shut and threw the bolt.

Then blew out a breath.

"That was way too close," he said, knowing with quick, brutal certainty that they would've been in serious trouble if the rioters had seen them. They were lucky they'd gotten away with that much of a sneak-and-peak.

Then again, with active fighting out the back door and Snake and his boys at the front, they were in pretty serious trouble as it was.

"We need to find someplace to hide," he whispered. "Someplace safe, with a sturdy door and a lock."

He was moments away from palming the flashlight and looking around when Gabby froze and squeezed his hand, hard. Moments later he heard it, too.

Footsteps crunched on glass, followed by the rattle of someone shaking the mangled storefront grate.

"Come out, come out, wherever you are," a voice called in high falsetto. "We don't want to hurt you."

But they would, Ty knew. Snake and his gang were hopped up on adrenaline and maybe something more.

As far as they were concerned, law had ceased existing when the power went out, and it was back to jungle rules. They wanted Gabby for some fun and games, but even more, they wanted his weapons. Without firearms, they couldn't stand up to the other, better-armed looters, which put them at the lowest rung of the hierarchy that'd taken over the south side of Boston.

Armed with knives and pipes, Snake and his crew were seriously dangerous. With the guns and thirty-plus rounds, they'd be looking for some serious trouble.

Part of Ty itched to get the drop on the kid and teach him a lesson he wouldn't soon forget. But he knew damn well that his priorities didn't include schooling wannabe gangbangers, so he urged Gabby to the side of the short hallway, where he could just make out a metal door with a knob and a dead-bolt lock.

"Stay behind me." He barely mouthed the words, but she understood, and managed to wedge herself between the wall and his body as he found the knob by touch and went to work.

Thanking the forethought that'd prompted him to slap on his web utility belt, he slipped a pair of thin, delicate metal strips from the belt and inserted them one at a time into the keyhole on the lock.

There was a time for kicking in doors, and this wasn't it. Thankfully, the instructors responsible for both his military and agency training had been unusually egalitarian in their methods, tempering brute force with practical clandestine skills like hot-wiring cars and picking locks.

He wasn't the best break-and-enter man he knew, though, and a prickle of sweat tickled his brow as the seconds ticked away and the jimmies slipped inside the locking mechanism. He could hear voices in the outer shop, cursing and muttering, along with several sets of footsteps. Had the whole gang followed them into the store? How had they known? Had they heard the noise? Had they—

"It's all gone," a plaintive voice whined from the front, and was echoed with a rising grumble of complaint. "Jeez, Snake, I thought you said there'd be food here."

"And I told you to quit your bitching and stop thinking about your stomach, for chrissake," the leader's voice snapped in return, sounding closer than Ty would've guessed, as though the bastard had already reached the corner near the hallway.

Come on, come on! He forced himself not to muscle the lock picks, knowing the key to the operation was feel rather than brute strength. His fingers itched for his guns, but that wasn't the right answer. Better to hide than kill a dozen men in front of Gabby and risk attracting ten times that many from the other side of the alley door.

"You sure you saw them duck in here?" It was Snake's voice again, muffled this time, as though he'd turned back to the main room.

There was a grumble, and Snake's voice sharpened

with annoyance. "Come on, people. Do I have to do every damn thing myself? Fan out. Check the other stores. And if you find food, don't forget I have first dibs. I'll finish checking this place and meet you on the street in fifteen."

Footsteps sounded nearby, crunching on chocolate wrappers and candy-covered peanuts.

Ty was seconds away from dropping the picks and going for his 9mm when the lock gave with a click. He breathed a sigh of relief and opened the door, forcing himself to move slowly when he wanted to hurry.

Silently, he guided Gabby into the room and then followed and pulled the door shut. He held his breath while he twisted the dead bolt on the inside, hoping to hell it wasn't the kind that engaged with a loud click. It wasn't, but the quiet snick of the lock sounded gunshot-loud to Ty, and from the tightening of Gabby's fingers where they dug into his upper arm, she thought so, too.

A quick, finger-shielded scan with the flashlight showed that they were in a small, windowless office with a desk against one wall and several filing cabinets against the other.

Once Ty had assured himself there was no other way in or out, he flicked off the light, lest a stray reflection give them away.

He held his breath and strained to hear Snake's footsteps out in the hallway, but the metal panel was too thick. That was both good and bad. Good because it'd be hell to kick in; bad because they had no idea what was going on in the hall.

Turning, he leaned close to Gabby, so his lips were close to her ear when he whispered on a puff of breath, "I can't hear him. Can you?"

"No," she whispered, equally quietly, tipping her head so she could speak into his ear, leaving them pressed cheek to cheek, wrapped together in the darkness. "I think we're safe in here."

Heat flared through Ty's body, and warning bells went off in the back of his brain as survival instincts told him to back off, to back away while he still could. But those alarms wound up buried beneath the feel of her, the feel of all those lush curves pressed against him, and the brush of her thick, glorious hair at his temple and jaw.

He inhaled, intending to push away from her, but the moment he caught her scent, that of woman and springtime laced with an overtone of the chocolate from the front room, a surge of lust punched through his system, swamping his defenses before he was even aware they were under attack. Or maybe he'd been aware all along, ever since she'd stepped out of the shadows and the woman he'd pretended to fall for online had become real.

And maybe, in a way, his pretend feelings had become real, too. Impossible, but real.

He was aware that she'd gone still against him, not even breathing. Her heartbeat was anything but still, though. He could feel the pounding at her throat, the pulse of heat and blood.

"Are you scared?" he asked quietly, aware of the gangbanger outside on one level, the woman beside him on another. There should've been no room for sex in the situation, no room for even the thought of it, but that was the heat that roared through him, and the heat he thought he caught off her.

"No," she said, equally quietly. "Or rather, yes, I'm scared, but at the same time I feel safe. With you."

"You shouldn't." His voice had gone rough. "I'm not feeling very safe right now."

He expected her to back off, to back away. Hell, he almost hoped she would, because it'd be the best thing for both of them if they walked away from the temptation now. But she'd stolen his will with a light touch of breath, freezing him in place and leaving the decision up to her.

Instead of backing away, she lifted her chin and turned her head so her lips grazed the sensitive skin beneath his jawline. "Then aren't we lucky the door locks on the inside?"

He had a flash of thinking her voice didn't sound right, that the light, teasing tone could've belonged to someone else, maybe the girl she'd been before the accident, or the woman she'd pretended to be online. It sounded false and unnatural, and that should've brought those alarm bells right to the forefront of his brain. But before the warning could sound, before he could pull back and figure out what the hell was going on and why he'd gotten involved with her when he'd planned on keeping his distance, she pressed her lips to the hollow beneath his ear, sending a whiplash of heat coiling through his midsection.

And he was lost.

Chapter Eight

Dear Ty:

I know you're not online, but just in case you get a chance to check your e-mail I wanted to wish you a happy Independence Day. You might not be in the military anymore—my friend Maria thinks it's totally hot that you're ex-Special Forces, by the way—but I'm guessing the Fourth is important to you. You're not the sort of guy who waves flags and joins parades, of course…but from what you've told me, I know your loyalty goes straight to the bone. And, wow, didn't this get heavy all of a sudden? Blame it on the first heat wave of the year here in Boston. Or maybe it's me. This is the first summer I was relieved when classes let out. At the same time, I'm restless. The prototype is almost done and I have a meeting with a patent agent, but I keep thinking to myself "this is it?" Ah…ignore me. I'm in a weird mood. Happy Fourth, and don't let any bad guys get at you or your boss. [Sent by CyberGabby; July 4, 11:01:42 p.m.]

3:00 a.m., August 3
2 Hour and 38 Minutes until Dawn

Gabby knew it was crazy—worse, it was stupid, given their situation—but she hadn't been able to stop herself from leaning into his solid body and wondering what if?

What if she hadn't gotten into Nathan's Camaro that night? What if they hadn't crashed? What if her parents had believed her about the headaches and blurry vision? What if the doctors had caught the problem earlier? *What if?*

She could no more stop the what-ifs from parading through her mind than she could keep herself from touching her lips to the strong column of Ty's neck, tasting salt, tasting man. She knew she was pushing the envelope, giving life to the wickedly impulsive girl inside her, the one who'd been responsible for all the bad things in her life.

But what if, this one time, those impulses could give her something good instead?

Thinking that, knowing it was impossible, she turned her lips to his.

Ty met her halfway.

The kiss was raw and openmouthed, buzzing with adrenaline and attraction, with the knowledge of safety in the small room and danger beyond. Heat flowed through her, threatening to consume her from the inside, spreading from the points where her body met his. Her breasts tightened to hard, wanting buds, and lust flared in her gut, warming and softening her inner muscles in an instant.

Stunned by the fierce, greedy response that was so unlike her normal staid self, Gabby nearly pulled back. *This isn't right,* she thought on a sudden slice of panic. *This is dangerous.*

But though the woman she'd grown into knew all the reasons she shouldn't return Ty's kiss, the inner party girl said otherwise, and somehow she'd gained the upper hand when Gabby hadn't been looking.

That wild, unpredictable, fun girl leaned into Ty, wrapped herself around him and hung on for the ride.

He slanted his mouth across hers and sucked gently, drawing her tongue into his mouth. Dark flavors assaulted her, mysterious and deep and vivid. Colors swirled across her consciousness, mimicking the flow of heat and sensation.

She touched her tongue to his and saw red sparkles on a hot-purple backdrop, slid her hands up the hard planes of his chest and saw a streak of royal blue. Her fingers found the edge of his shoulder holster. Tracing the leather and nylon straps, she added the weapon to her mental image of him.

Oddly, though she'd known he was armed, she hadn't thought of the guns when she'd pictured him. She hadn't thought of the darkness across the city, or of whether he wore a badge or carried cuffs. Her mental image had been set by his first online description, with too-long blond hair flopping into his eyes and a too-infrequent smile.

Now, touching him, she added reality to the mental picture, added the feel of him, the taste of him and the beat of his heart.

She'd never been one of those people who "saw" others by touching their faces. To her, noses, jaws and lips all felt the same. At least they had before.

Now, touching Ty and burying her fingers in his thick hair, she felt the faint wave in the soft strands. Cupping his face in her hands, she felt the squareness of his jaw and his high, slashing cheekbones. Drawing her fingers down the column of his neck, across his broad, muscular shoulders to his strong arms, she envisioned the man she was coming to know.

And in seeing the reality, she teetered a little close to the edge of falling.

They strained together, kissing, touching, breathing the same air. Wonder shimmered through her alongside fear, and this time the fear won out.

Not by much, though. Her heart pounded in her chest and she was breathing hard; they both were. Her blood buzzed with heat and lust, and her head drummed with the mad, insane compulsion to keep kissing him, to go further, to damn the consequences and become lovers though they barely knew each other, and danger was mere feet away.

It was that very danger that compelled her, she knew. It drew her. It commanded her. It made her do stupid things that felt so good at the time, then lived on to haunt her. Like this.

But is this so wrong? she thought on a sudden spurt of defiance, and deliberately took the kiss deeper, sliding her hands down to touch his heavy equipment belt and the taut muscles of his abdomen. Was it wrong to take something now, something she could hold on to and remember later, not with shame, but with the thrill of flesh on flesh?

In a few hours it would be over one way or the other, and she and Ty would part for good. What harm was there in taking what she wanted now?

He tore his mouth away and pressed his forehead to hers, his ribs heaving. "Gabby." He kissed her as though he was helpless to do otherwise, as though the same mad impulse rode him as well. "I think—" He broke off and shuddered against her as she raked her fingernails beneath his shirt, up and across the taut muscles of his chest. "Geez."

"Here." She took his hand and held it so they untied her knotted shirt together, giving him access, giving him permission and a demand all at once. His breath hissed out, then hers did, as well, when he used both hands to cup her breasts and rub her nipples to points beneath a bra she'd chosen with him in mind, though she'd had no illusions they would even meet, let alone come so far so fast.

Fast. The word echoed in her mind, trying to slow her down when she wanted to race ahead, wanted to feel the wind screaming through the T-tops of a hot rod once again. But she didn't want to be slow anymore, didn't want to be cautious.

What she wanted was Ty, here and now. And fast.

She went to work on his pants, where the material felt slick to her fingers, like the fine wool of a suit or maybe a tuxedo. His shirt, too, had the ridged gathers of formal wear. Remembering that he'd been at a formal party just before the blackout, and she added a tuxedo to the image in her mind, with devastating effect.

"Let me," he said, when her fingers went to her waistband, and then, "Are you sure?"

"Check my back pocket and see for yourself." She didn't have to tell him it had been a joke, Maria being silly about what might happen when they went to their late-night rendezvous. They'd laughed about the condom, and Gabby had kept it as a sort of talisman, as though by carrying it she could pretend a little longer that what she and Ty had built together was real.

Only, it had become real when she wasn't looking. TyJ had become Ty to her, a flawed and imperfect man with a loose grasp on the truth and a stubborn streak a mile wide. And somehow none of that seemed to matter when it came to the way she felt about him.

She liked him. She wanted him. Couldn't it be as simple as that?

His fingers found the small foil packet, and his breath hissed between his teeth. She shimmied out of the rest of her clothing "What do you say?" she asked, and slid a hand inside the warmth within his tuxedo pants, finding him hard and ready. She thrilled to his hiss of indrawn breath, and the jump of his shaft beneath her touch.

"I say hell, yes." He boosted her up onto the desk, sheathed himself in the condom and stepped between her knees. Then he lowered his head and kissed her deeply, searchingly, until there was a thread of tenderness coiling alongside the heat. Then he pulled away, he pressed his forehead to hers. "I know this isn't the right time or place, and I'm sure as hell not the right man, but I can't make any of that matter right now."

With his forehead still pressed to hers, he stepped into her until the blunt tip of his shaft nudged against her opening, a tantalizing pressure she'd taken for granted during one part of her life and gone without during the other.

"Ty," she breathed, loving the feel of him against her, the sound of his name on her lips.

"Gabby," he said, responding in kind as he eased forward and slid home.

She felt that first wonderful, glorious burn of invasion, then the warm glow as her body adjusted to the size and shape of him, to the reality of him. In that moment she felt feminine. She felt beautiful. She felt whole.

And then he began to move, and everything else ceased to exist.

He thrust into her and withdrew, urging her to the edge of the desk and cupping her buttocks with his warm hands, holding her fast as he surged into her again, stretching her, filling her.

Gabby fisted her hands in his finely woven shirt, threw back her head and hung on for the ride as he thrust into her again and again, the tempo increasing, the sensations increasing, layering one atop the next until she thought she might scream with the pleasure.

Instead she wrapped herself around him, leaned forward and pressed her mouth to his shoulder, silencing the cries that threatened to break from her.

They strained together in silence broken only by the noise of their breathing and the slap of flesh. The sound was brutally erotic, coiling the heat inside her higher and higher until she tightened around him. The orgasm was a sharp, vicious slice of pleasure that cut straight through her and left her shuddering, gasping and not quite settled inside her own skin.

Then Ty stiffened against her and she felt him swell inside her, felt his hard flesh jerk with his release, setting a rhythm that echoed within her, calling to the unsettled energy and bringing the whiplash of a second, unexpected climax.

This time she did cry out, a little moan that she quickly muffled against his hot flesh.

Ty sagged against her, barely breathing. He slid his hands out from beneath her and held her tight, held her against him so hard it seemed as if they had become a single unit, their hearts beating in tandem, their flesh fused until it was difficult to tell where one of them left off and the other began.

They stayed like that for a long moment, then pulled apart without a word.

Swaying slightly with vertigo, Gabby dropped her feet to the floor and pulled on her clothes with trembling fingers.

"Wow," she whispered, her voice breaking on the word, on the sensations still rocketing through her body. "That was amazing."

"Yes. Yes, it was." His voice rasped deep in his throat, and she thought she caught a hint of emotion in his voice. Regret, perhaps, or maybe something softer. Instead of saying it never should have happened, or any of the hundred excuses that flashed through her brain in a nanosecond, he simply said, "Thank you."

Her lips curved. "The pleasure was mine."

"I think we can safely say it was mutual." He dealt with the condom and righted his clothing, and then she heard the rasp of metal on leather that was becoming all too familiar. "Speaking of safety, we don't know what's going to be on the other side of that door when we open it. I want you to take this."

He pressed the warm plastic grip of one of his guns into her palm.

Gabby's fingers instinctively curled around the gun even as she said, "No way. Don't even think about it." Shock had her words coming out far louder than she'd intended, far louder than was wise.

They both froze as the sound echoed in the small room, but there was no response from outside.

There was only silence.

After a moment Ty exhaled. "Well, that's a good sign at any rate. Maybe they're gone." But she noticed that he kept his voice to a bare whisper. He gripped her shoulders, wordlessly urging her to the side of the door. Then he stood behind her and reached around to position her hands on the gun. He rubbed her index finger across a small nub and whispered, "That's the safety. This is on. This is off. Rack the action like this." As he demonstrated, she was all too aware of the feel of his arms around her, and the hard planes of his chest pressed against her back, echoing their embrace of moments earlier. "Keep your finger outside the trigger guard until you plan on firing," he continued. "And when you pull the trigger make sure you mean it."

She shifted to whisper in his ear, "You do remember I can't see, right?"

He dropped his arms and moved away from her,

leaving her skin to cool where they'd been pressed together. His voice went deadly serious when he said, "I don't know what's on the other side of that door. I want you to be protected in case…just in case."

A shiver crawled across Gabby's shoulders. Instead of insisting he take the weapon back, she tightened her fingers on the grip, keeping the index finger of her right hand stretched out beside the trigger guard as he'd shown her. "Okay. Thanks."

She didn't intend to fire the gun, but the weight gave her an odd sense of confidence.

"I'm going to open the door on the count of three," he whispered. "If anyone's out there, I'll do my best to get the door closed." He didn't follow with the logical corollary—that the door would only keep them out for so long. Instead he said, "I'll try to let you know where I am and what's going on. If I go down—" He broke off, and she sensed him moving closer, felt his warmth on her skin when he said, "Never mind. We're going to get out of here in one piece."

But she noticed that he didn't make any promises.

She nodded. "I'm ready."

He hesitated momentarily and she thought he might kiss her, thought he might call her sweetheart.

Instead he turned away.

FOCUS, FOR CHRISSAKES. Ty forced himself to reach for the doorknob rather than the woman who stood beside him. Then he paused and took a deep breath. He had to focus, had to get hold of himself. What was it about her that distracted him so easily, derailed him so thoroughly?

Whatever it was, it was dangerous. He'd never meant to kiss her, never meant to give in to the temptation and make love to her, but all his best intentions hadn't stood a chance against the feel of her, the taste of her, hell, against *her*.

He'd come damn close to falling for her online, when he'd been pretending to be someone else, someone kind. Now he was teetering even closer to that edge, and that made it even more vital that he step the hell away from her and pull it together.

If anything happened to her... *No,* he thought fiercely. *I won't let anything happen to her.*

Then again he'd promised to protect Mandy, and look how that had ended up.

"Here goes nothing," he said, trying to sound confident for Gabby's benefit, but carrying a knot in his gut as he slowly unlocked the dead bolt with one hand, holding his revolver at the ready with the other. He opened the door in one smooth move, stepped through and swept the short hallway from one end to the other, finger already on the trigger.

His adrenaline was buzzing so high it took him a moment to register that the hallway was empty.

Exhaling an almost shaky breath, he whispered, "Clear so far."

It was clear the rest of the way out, too, though he hardly dared believe their luck. At the same time, he was cursing himself for the delay. God only knew how long Snake and his boys had been gone.

Ty would've known, too, except he'd been making love to exactly the sort of woman he'd made it a habit to avoid. She was the home-and-hearth type, the type who'd want him home every night. More important, she was the type who needed more from him than he was capable of giving. He needed his freedom. She needed a partner. Complete disconnect.

"Come on," he said, not whispering now. His voice came out gruff with anger, not at her, but at himself. He knew better, damn it. What had gotten into him?

That question was answered moments later, when he flicked on the flashlight and saw her standing in the hallway, her hair falling down around her shoulders in glorious disarray, looking as though she'd just climbed out of a man's bed. *Not any man's bed*, Ty thought with a territorial surge of possessiveness that undermined all his vows of moments earlier. *My bed.*

She was gripping his Glock two-handed in a position that should've been intimidating, but as far as Ty was concerned looked pinup sexy.

Damn, was he in trouble.

He could try to talk himself out of it as much as he might like, but she'd gotten under his skin long before they'd met face-to-face.

"It's getting late," she said, forcing him back on track. "I think we should risk a car."

"My thoughts exactly," he lied. "I'll take that back if you don't mind." He snagged the gun, checked the safety and holstered the weapon. "Come on."

He took her hand, shaded the flashlight with his free hand so only a tiny beam of light emerged, and led her through the front room of the candy store, which showed new evidence of vandalism.

Snake and his boys had upended the remaining tables and smashed the remaining display case on their way out, looking for food, maybe, or entertainment.

Knowing that fledgling gangs tended not to stray far from their territories, Ty stayed alert as they left the store and headed east, back toward the waterfront. They stuck to the shadows and moved fast, hustling away from the swath of destroyed homes and businesses as quickly as possible.

Once they were clear of the looted area, he unshielded the light and shone the beam in a wide arc, gauging the neighborhood. The brick row houses were similar to those farther south, but they were in far better repair, and the cars lining either curb were mostly late-model sedans and SUVs.

Best of all, the street was clear of wrecks and abandoned vehicles.

"Nicer neighborhoods get National Guard action sooner than the scary ones," he noted.

"It smells cleaner." Gabby tested the air. "Less smoke, too. No looting?"

"Not here." Ty scanned the street again, checking for motion behind the pitch-dark windows, then made his choice. He decided on a low-slung gray car with familiar smooth lines. "Come on." He tugged her toward the vehicle, pulled a flexible cat's paw tool from his belt and went to work on the driver's-side window.

"You're not doing what I think you're doing, are you?"

Ty chuckled at her dry tone. "If I don't tell you, then you're not really an accomplice to grand theft auto, are you?"

"And that was not telling me how?" Gabby took advantage of the brief delay to rummage through his knapsack for a chocolate bar.

By the time she got it unwrapped, Ty had the car unlocked. He opened the driver's door, leaned over and popped the lock on the other side. "You want to walk to the medical center?"

"No," she said firmly. "We don't have enough time." She picked up the knapsack and headed for the passenger's side, trailing her free hand along the length of the hood. As she did so, a faint frown puckered the smooth skin between her eyebrows.

At the mention of time, Ty glanced at his watch and cursed. "We're going to be cutting it close. Let's get a move on." He swung into the driver's seat and went to work on the steering column, cracking it to expose the relevant wires, stripping them and crossing them in under a minute.

When he had the car started, he looked up to find Gabby still standing in the doorway on the opposite side of the vehicle with her hand on the T-top roof of the classic car he'd chosen because he'd take an old-fashioned hot rod over an SUV any day.

Gabby's face was ghost white.

It took him a few seconds, but then he remembered what she'd told Kayleigh. *We were racing a souped-up Camaro with a T-top...we missed the turn...hit a minivan...flipped end over end.*

"Oh, hell. I forgot." Ty couldn't believe he'd forgotten. Or maybe the car choice had been a dig from his subconscious. Who the hell knew? What was done was done. "I'm sorry, sweetheart." The endearment slipped out unbidden, just as the urge to comfort her came out of nowhere, unwanted and unwise.

She swallowed miserably, but got a glint of fight in her eyes. "Then you *were* listening to me and Kayleigh back at the halfway house. I thought so." She lifted one shoulder, but the haunted expression didn't drain. "Saves me the trouble of going through it again if you wanted to know how it happened."

Ty stopped himself from saying that of course he wanted to know, because he didn't have the right. He couldn't give her what she needed, which meant he didn't get to pretend that they were still TyJ and CyberGabby, that they were feeling their way into a relationship.

So instead of asking about the accident, or her parents, or what she'd done when the doctors gave her the news, or all the hundred other things he wanted to know about her, he said, "I'm sorry, but we don't have time to jack another car."

"I know." She took a deep breath, lowered herself into the vehicle and strapped herself in, handling the three-point harness with ease. Then she closed the door firmly and nodded. "Let's go."

WHEN SHE'D FIRST realized what sort of car Ty had boosted, Gabby had thought she was going to throw up again. When she'd climbed inside, she'd nearly done exactly that. But the moment Ty hit the gas, sending them flying out onto the street, everything changed.

Oh God, she thought as they rocketed forward, and inertia pressed her back against the seat. *I've missed this.*

She hadn't missed riding in cars one bit. But now she realized she'd missed riding in fast, mean cars with engines that sounded like a dragon's roar.

"It's not going to take long for someone to notice us." She heard Ty rummage around for a second, then felt him press a cell phone and charger into her hand. "Here, plug this in, will you?"

"What? Oh, sure." Rousted from street-racing flashbacks, Gabby did as he'd said, only fumbling momentarily before she managed to hook up the phone.

Within moments it dinged with a ready chime, indicating that it had both power and a signal, though she couldn't have said how strong that signal actually was.

"Dial for me, will you?" He reeled off a number. "You'll have to do the talking. I'm running without lights here, and I'd rather not multitask."

"You're running without—God, I don't think I wanted to know that." Gabby winced, shut up and dialed the number. "It's ringing."

"Say a prayer it doesn't dump to voice mail. I text messaged Dana and told her to have Ethan snag some charge on his cell for a 4:00 a.m. call."

Gabby raised a brow. "What happened to not contacting the authorities?"

"Dana and Ethan aren't with the Secret Service. We're—" Ty broke off. "They're friends."

Something prickled at the base of her spine when she realized that deep down inside, she knew he was lying. "Friends."

"Yep," Ty said shortly. "No answer?"

Another lie, followed by an evasion. What was going on here?

Gabby knew her voice sounded thin when she said, "No answer. No voice mail, either, which might mean the whole system is—"

She broke off when the line clicked live and a man's voice said, "Hello?"

"Hello," she said automatically, then faltered and hissed at Ty, "Somebody answered. What am I supposed to tell him?"

"Who is this?" The stranger's voice sharpened with immediate suspicion.

"I'm calling for Ty Jones," she said, though he probably knew that from caller ID. "My name is Gabby."

"Oh," the stranger said, then more slowly, as though he knew who she was, "Oh, really? Is he there?"

"He's driving." More accurately, he was flying, taking the corners on two wheels with a scream of protest from the rubber they were laying down. Gabby leaned in to the turn and wished she could simply sit back and enjoy.

How could she have forgotten this part?

"Tell Ethan we need a distraction," Ty bit out between reverse loops of a snaking turn. "We need the cops and the Guard otherwise occupied while we make a run to Boston General. And ask him if he can keep the phone on. I have a feeling that's not our final destination."

"I heard him," Ethan, said before Gabby could relay the questions. "Give us ten minutes to take care of the distraction. And yes, I'll keep the phone on as long as I can. Where the hell are we supposed to meet him? Near the hospital?"

She parroted the question, but Ty said only, "I'll call

him. Tell him to stay the hell away from the hospital, but be ready to move fast."

"Got it," Ethan said. "I don't like it, but I've got it." His voice shifted. "Are you two okay?"

"For now," Gabby said, confused that he was talking to her like he knew who she was and what she was doing with Ty. Or were his friends used to him picking up women and dragging them into situations like this?

Somehow she didn't think so.

"We'll be waiting to hear from you. And, Gabby?"

"Yes?" Her head was starting to spin, and she didn't think it was from the speed or the chocolate buzz.

"Take care of him for us, okay? He's not nearly as tough as he wants everybody to think."

Ethan hung up, leaving Gabby even more confused than she'd been moments earlier.

"What'd he say?"

"He said to give them ten minutes before you try to reach the hospital, and after that, they'd wait for you to call." She kept the rest of the conversation to herself. What had Ethan meant? Why had he told her such a thing? He'd seemed to know who she was, had seemed to accept her presence without question. Had he thought she was someone else, or had Ty mentioned her at some point?

And if so, why? Why would he have talked about a woman he was pretending to romance as part of a

Secret Service inquiry? Had he laughed about it, or was there something else going on?

Without warning, Ty hit the brakes, cut the wheel and killed the engine.

The silence and stillness was a shock in the wake of the roar and power of the Camaro, and Gabby nearly gasped. "What is it? What's wrong?"

"We've got company up ahead—three Guard transpos and a tank. Cross your fingers that Ethan and the others come through pronto with that distraction. Until then, we'll have to lay low and make like an abandoned car."

He didn't suggest they hunker down in the foot-wells, probably because it was still so dark out. Gabby was thankful for the small reprieve, because the moment they stopped moving the shivers returned, reminding her of all the bad things that could happen in fast cars driven by hot men.

Looking to distract herself, she said, "You keep mentioning others, but you said they weren't Secret Service. What are you, part of some black-ops unit or something?"

He chuckled. "You've been watching too many movies."

"TV, mostly," she said, registering the evasion. "I like to listen to it while I work on the computers." Which only served to remind her of what'd happened back at the apartment—her computers had been broken, her 3-

D tactile imaging prototype destroyed, her space violated. The thought should've depressed her.

The fact that it didn't was almost worse.

What was happening to her settled, comfortable way of life?

Suddenly, practical Gabby and the North End seemed very far away.

"We'll get you home soon," Ty said, misreading her completely. "My friend Shane is a wizard with computers. I'll have him take a look and see what you can salvage."

"Don't condescend," she snapped, as the shivers turned into something else, something more raw and volatile. "I built them, I can fix them. That's what I do." Angry tears suddenly threatened as her frustrations piled up one atop the next. "I'm blind, not incapable."

He was silent for a moment, then said very carefully, "I don't remember saying you were."

"You didn't need to say it. I know very well you wouldn't have gotten involved with me if you'd known I can't see." A vicious ache gathered in her chest. "That's right. You were under orders to get involved, weren't you? Orders handed down by your friend Grant Davis, hero, patriot and friend to Boston's needy."

She knew that was aiming low, and wasn't sure she cared. She wanted to pick a fight, wanted to yell at him, wanted him to yell back and give her a good reason not to want him, a good reason to walk the hell away and not look back, so she'd be the one leaving this time rather than him.

But before he could answer, three dull thuds sounded in the distance, vibrating through the very earth itself.

Ty started the Camaro and said tightly, "That's our distraction, and there goes the Guard." He shifted into gear. "Hang on. It's going to be a bumpy ride."

Chapter Nine

Hey, Gabs:

You know what I think? I think you should take a weekend away. Just pack a few things and get out of the city. Maybe Maria would go with you? Forgive me if I don't suggest bringing a guy friend along. I know I said I wasn't the jealous type, and it's probably selfish of me—heck, I *know* it's selfish—but I like the idea of having you to myself, even if it's just online. Maybe one of these days you'll come clean on why you don't want to meet me. Is it the fear that the fantasy wouldn't be as good as what we've built up here in cyber-space? Or is it something else entirely? I'm betting on the "something else," because, baby, I can assure you that I'm even better in person than I am online.

I guess what I'm trying to say is…I really think we should meet. What's the worst that could happen?

[Sent by TyJ; July 15, 1:05:25 a.m.]

4:12 a.m., August 3
1 Hour and 26 Minutes until Dawn

When the members of Eclipse did a job it got done right, so Ty flipped on the Camaro's headlights and kept the pedal to the metal all the way across the city, trusting that he was clear.

But although the road was empty, he was far from clear.

"I'm sorry," he said through gritted teeth. "I was only trying to help."

She sighed. "And I was trying to pick a fight. So I'm sorry, too."

Her apology didn't fix things, though. If anything, it worsened the tension in his gut and the pounding ache in his chest, the one that told him he was on the edge of a dangerous drop, leaning out toward empty space.

As the darkened city blocks flew past on either side of them, he said, "You know I was married to my high school sweetheart. Mandy."

He kept his eyes front, but felt her surprise and heard it in her voice when she said, "You mentioned her once or twice." She paused. "I take it the divorce was ugly?"

Ty knew it had to be said, knew it would explain things she wouldn't understand otherwise. Still, it took an effort of will for him to say, "There was no divorce. She died of a brain aneurysm while I was overseas."

He kept his eyes on the road, but he heard her hiss

of indrawn breath. She was quiet for a couple of blocks before she sighed. "Another lie."

"If I told you it was the last one, would you believe me?"

"Only if you promised," she said, tone ringing with quiet dignity.

"It's a promise, then. I won't lie to you again." He wanted to reach out to her, to touch her in some way and make her understand, but she seemed so very far away on her side of the hot rod. So instead, he said, "I think I told you that Mandy and I argued about my work schedule. Quite a bit, in fact. She wanted me home more, wanted me to make more of a commitment to our marriage. We were…" He trailed off. Exhaled. "We were together for six months after I got out of the military, before I proposed. I thought it was long enough for us to get to know each other again, long enough to be sure it was right. It turned out a relationship can make it through six months on not much more than memories and inertia."

She glanced at him now. "You were thinking of divorcing?"

"No," he said quickly, then, "maybe. I don't know. We were crazy about each other, but we weren't doing very well living with each other. She thought I should quit the Secret Service and take a security position closer to where we grew up, so she could be near her family when we decided to have kids. She didn't understand that back then…" His throat closed on the memory, on something close to panic. "That was eight years ago, and I wasn't ready to slow down yet. Hell, even the protection detail wasn't enough action for me. I wanted to be on the front lines again, wanted to be making a difference where it counted."

"You wanted to be a hero," Gabby said softly. She'd turned back to him, but her expression was still closed. Suspicious.

"I'm no hero. Never have been." Ty stared straight ahead into the darkness, gripping the Camaro's steering wheel so tightly his fingers ached. "I volunteered for a special assignment and wound up getting sent abroad on almost no notice." That had been the beginning of Eclipse, the very first assignment for a band of brothers who'd all grown bored with civilian life and had gone looking for a challenge. It had also been Mandy's birthday. He blew out a breath and kept going. "We were supposed to meet at a restaurant that evening. She'd called me up earlier in the day to say she wasn't sure about dinner, that she wasn't feeling well."

He'd been relieved by that, which made it worse somehow. He'd thought if she postponed the birthday dinner for a few days and they celebrated when he got back from that first mission, it'd be okay. It wouldn't be him bailing on her, wouldn't be him being unavailable.

Except he'd been exactly that—gone when she'd needed him most.

He wasn't aware that he'd fallen silent, lost in bad memories and guilt, until Gabby said, "What happened?"

"I got the call the moment I stepped off the plane. She'd died of an aneurysm. The damned headache killed her." *I killed her,* he wanted to say, but didn't because he couldn't bear hearing the logic of the arguments against it. He should've been with her. It'd been her birthday, damn it. He should've been there, and if he had been, he would've figured out how badly she was hurting, and he would've dragged her to the E.R.

The doctors had said if they'd caught the bleed early enough, surgery probably would have saved her life. As it was, she'd died all alone in their bedroom.

In a silence broken only by the muttering rumble of the Camaro's engine, Ty waited for Gabby's pity, for her understanding.

Instead she turned away from him and pressed her cheek to the window. "How much farther to Boston General?"

On any other day, with any other person, Ty told himself he would've appreciated not having to fend off the sympathy. With Gabby, though, the withdrawal stung.

It was no more than he deserved, but he realized on some level he'd expected more. He'd wanted more, which was damned unfair of him, given that he wasn't willing to give anything back.

Muttering a curse, he gripped the steering wheel

even harder and sent them hurtling into the night. "Not far now. Not long until dawn, either."

By the time the sun rose over Boston, things would be over, one way or the other. Either he'd save Grant Davis and be a hero, or Grant would be dead and part of Boston leveled. Regardless of how it went down, there was one unavoidable fact.

When the dawn came, TyJ and CyberGabby would be going their separate ways.

TRUE TO HIS WORD—this one, at least—Ty pulled the Camaro over and threw it into Park within a few minutes, but those minutes had dragged endlessly for Gabby.

Just when she'd started to believe she knew Ty, just when she'd started to think there were no more secrets, no more surprises between them, he'd cracked and told her the truth about Mandy. The confidence should've felt like progress. Instead, it felt like a huge step backward off a fatal drop.

The faint, sad echo in his voice when he spoke of his ex wasn't because of a painful divorce. It was true sadness, mixed with guilt. And if she'd thought once or twice that she could compete with a bad ex, there was no way in hell she could compete with a dead woman.

Besides, what could she offer Ty besides more of the same? She'd worry just as hard if her man were overseas on some black-ops mission—and as much as he might try to pretend he wasn't black-ops, she wasn't an idiot. And although she'd worked hard to become as self-sufficient as possible, she needed help sometimes. Right now the onus fell on Maria. At one point, she'd hoped to find a man to share the burden with her, but time and experience had proven that was impossible.

Even more so with a vital, physically active man like Ty.

"Come on," he said now, and she heard the Camaro's door swing open. "Stick close to me. After what we found at the halfway house, I'm not sure what to expect here."

It'd only been an hour or so since they'd left Tom and Lennie's house, but to Gabby it felt like days. So much had happened in the interim—the gang, the chase, hiding out in the office, making love to Ty on a stranger's desk…. God, she almost felt like a different person than the one who'd sat and talked to Kayleigh, and she definitely felt a whole world away from the woman who'd hidden in the bushes while Maria pretended to be her.

Problem was, she might be a different person now, but she had no idea who that person was.

Emerging from the Camaro, she paused and frowned as the sounds and smells didn't line up with what she'd been expecting. "I thought you said the last campaign stop was Boston General."

"Not the hospital itself." He joined her on the curb and took her hand, but instead of curling his fingers against hers, he guided her grip to his belt. "We're at one of the administration buildings on the Mass Ave. side of the hospital. We had a thousand-dollar-a-plate luncheon here, where Grant gave a speech promising to work on health care reform, giving it a more global-ized context and making high-quality care more ac-cessible for the working class."

"That sounds pretty vague." Gabby tilted her head, trying to predict the next move. "It'd be hard for Liam to prove he went back on those promises."

"If that's what he's trying to do." Ty's voice was tight, warning her not to push the issue. "I'm inclined to think he's just playing an elaborate game with us, that he never intended to tell me where the bomb is, or give me an opportunity to defuse it and rescue Grant."

But that didn't stop him from heading for the admin building, tugging Gabby along in his wake. She stumbled a little on tired legs, but followed Ty out of habit as much as anything.

Deep inside her a seed of resentment took root and began to grow. She didn't want to be here, didn't want to be a part of this.

"I don't belong here," she said quietly, her heart breaking a little. "I'm not helping you at all. If anything, I'm slowing you down just like I said I would. Let me go home. Please."

She could feel the frustration and impatience radi-ating off Ty. Because of it, she half expected him to snap at her or, hell, even agree and call one of his "not Secret Service" friends to come get her.

Instead he turned, wrapped his arms around her and held her close, resting his cheek against the top of her head. "I'm sorry, sweetheart."

Thoroughly undone by the unexpected tenderness, by the odd feeling that he needed the contact as much as she did at that moment, Gabby froze, not sure how to react.

"I wish things had been different," he said. "I wish I really were a corporate bodyguard, and that I'd picked your photo out because I liked your hair and your gorgeous smile. I wish I were really in a position to have a girlfriend or a wife and have it be fair for both of us. Most of all, I wish I hadn't dragged you into this. I wish you were safe at home, that your computers weren't broken, that the lights were on, that none of this had happened…" He trailed off and she heard him sigh. "Only that's a lie, too, because I can't wish I'd never met you in person. You're so damn much more than you seem, more even than you're ready to believe."

Tired of the push-pull between them, tired of the night and the darkness, Gabby drew away. "I'm sorry, Ty. I can't—"

He silenced her with a kiss.

Unprepared, she parted her lips in shock, and Ty must have taken that as an invitation to deepen the kiss, cupping her hips in his hands and urging her closer to his bulk.

The kiss was brief but no less intense for its brevity, and they were both breathing hard when he eased back and said, "No, I'm the one who's apologizing here, not you. I'm sorry I can't promise to be what you need, and I'm sorry I can't seem to make that matter right now."

This time she pushed all the way away from him and took a step back. She shook her head. "None of this matters right now, Ty, and we both know it. Let's focus on finding your Patriot. After that, if you want, we can take some time and figure out if there's anything between us besides lies, bad timing and some sparks."

His silence over the next few heartbeats spoke volumes, confirming what she already knew deep in her gut.

There was no future for them beyond the dawn.

Finally he said, "Come on. Grant's podium was set up over here." This time he took her hand in his, but his grip was an impersonal clasp rather than an intimate finger twine.

As they crossed the pavement, their footsteps echoed off a high wall on one side of them. Gabby trailed her free hand along the surface and identified a building sided with brick veneer, meaning that it was newer construction than the real brick facings in the North End. When Ty reversed direction, forcing them to retrace their steps, and then did a second about-face, she said, "You're not seeing anything?"

"Nothing," he said, voice harsh with bitterness.

"What if this has all been a wild-goose chase? What if Liam was just killing time, running me around in circles while he—" He broke off. "Wait a second. I think I see something."

"What is it?"

"Wait here." He pulled away abruptly, and Gabby heard him hurry forward a few steps.

Leaving her standing alone.

TY CROUCHED DOWN and aimed his flashlight toward a shadowed doorway, where a glint of reflected light had caught his attention.

"Gotcha," he breathed in triumph. A small gray detonator cap sat atop a folded piece of paper. He gave a quick scan for trip wires and booby traps, then lifted the cap for a quick inspection.

It was a standard military design, a multifunctional detonator that could be used with a dozen different explosives and hundreds of designs. Not much of a clue.

"Hopefully, this is something better." He reached down and snagged the paper. Unfolding it, he quickly scanned the handwritten note.

You always were loyal to a fault, Jones, which was part of why I liked you. I'm sorry it has to be this way, but I need you to listen to me. Meet me at the entrance to the Ted Williams Tunnel, and come alone. If you're not there by 5:00, or if you bring company, both of them are dead.

"Both of them?" Ty said aloud. "What do you think he means by—"

He broke off and spun toward where he'd left Gabby. She was gone.

Ty's heart stopped, simply stopped in his chest. One moment she'd been standing there, waiting for him, the emotions of their conversation, of their situation, written plainly on her lovely face.

Then the next minute, *poof*. She was gone.

He surged to his feet on a roar of pain, of frustration. *"Liam Shea!"*

There was no answer save for the low throb of sirens in the distance. Then, closer by, he heard a car engine fire up, followed by a squeal of tires.

"Damn it!" Ty bolted toward the Camaro, which still sat with both doors hanging open. He slammed the passenger's door and ran around to the driver's side, but once he was inside the vehicle, he banged his fists into the steering wheel and cursed viciously.

He'd turned his back on her for only seconds, maybe a minute, tops, but it'd been long enough for Liam to take her. For what?

A lure? A threat? A diversion?

"I don't know what the hell you want from me, you bastard," Ty snarled, but he knew what he had to do next. He had to get to the entrance to the Ted Williams Tunnel, and a quick check of his watch warned that he had roughly twenty minutes to do it.

He fired the engine and hit the gas, sending the Camaro screaming out into the night, and though he wasn't a praying man, he found a litany running through his brain as he drove.

Please, God, let her be okay.

Chapter Ten

Dear Ty:
I know you don't understand why I won't meet you, and I know you're hurt that I keep refusing. I can only say that I'm sorry. Over the past four months, your friendship has meant more to me than you'll ever know. You've reminded me of things I'd forgotten I cared about, and you've made me wish that things could be different, more than any other person has ever done. However, what we have now is all we can ever have. I hope you can respect that while still being, at the very least, my friend.
[Sent by CyberGabby; July 25, 3:32:06 p.m.]

4:45 a.m., August 3
53 Minutes until Dawn

Gabby woke with pain screaming through her head, panic not far behind.

She was lying on her side, her legs and arms bent

and sending pinfire pain from loss of circulation. She groaned and tried to stretch out, but banged against metal walls. Engine noise sounded all around her, and the stink of exhaust crinkled her sinuses as the roughly carpeted surface beneath her jolted, wringing another groan out of her when she reached the only possible conclusion that made any sense. Terrifying sense.

She was in the trunk of Liam's car.

"Oh, God." She didn't remember being grabbed. The last thing she remembered was…fighting with Ty, she supposed. They'd been in the car, headed for the hospital, and he'd been telling her about Mandy, giving her a subtext that had been all too clear.

Don't be thinking about happily ever after just because we kissed. I like being on my own and making my own schedule, and there isn't room in my life for a woman.

He hadn't said "for a woman like you," but she'd heard the words. They were the same words Jeff hadn't said when he'd broken up with her, deciding she was just too much work for not enough reward.

"Jerks," she said aloud, boosting the volume to give herself a jolt of confidence. "I. Am. Not. An. Invalid!"

Nobody said you were, a small voice reminded her from deep inside, giving her a moment's pause, a moment to wonder if she was reading something that wasn't there after all.

Then the driver decelerated and downshifted, and

the vehicle hooked a sharp left. Gabby's eyes teared and her stomach clenched as she forced herself to face the fact that she was in far more trouble than just a bad first date.

She'd been kidnapped by a madman bent on revenge.

"Think, Gabby," she said aloud. What would Ty want her to do in the situation? What would she have done as a wily teenager? She used to be able to slip past any curfew, escape from any locked house, past every watchful parental eye.

What would that girl have done?

When there was no answer from deep inside, a tear broke free and trickled across her cheek. Oh, God, what was she supposed to do? How was she supposed to get herself out of this?

The vehicle stopped abruptly, brakes squealing. Inertia flung her backward and she slammed into something hard and sharp. She cried out in pain, the shriek sounding unnaturally loud in the closed-in space.

The engine died, and moments later, a car door slammed and heavy footsteps approached the rear of the vehicle.

Gabby squeezed her eyelids tightly shut and felt tears leak from beneath them. She tried to swipe them away, only then realizing that her wrists were tied in front of her, connected with a short length of rope that let her move some, but not much. She scissored her legs and found that her ankles were similarly bound.

Helpless, she could only flinch when the trunk lid clicked and opened, and a man's voice said, "Good, you're awake. This'll make things easier."

She recognized Liam's voice from Christ Church, but before she could ask what was happening or where he'd taken her, he grabbed her roughly by both arms, hauled her up and out of the trunk and dragged her out into the unknown.

TY CUT THROUGH Chinatown, knowing it was a gamble with its narrow, twisty streets that might not have been cleared yet, but also knowing it was the quickest way through. He made it—barely—through a bottleneck formed between a wall and a graffiti-covered delivery truck lying on its side, then hit the gas and sent the Camaro flying straight across Commercial Street…

And into the side of a tank.

Ty saw the gray-green bulk too late to turn, too late to do anything but shout and brace himself.

The Camaro hit hard, its front end crumpling into a mess of metal and fiberglass, its windshield spider-webbing and sagging inward. The impact snapped Ty against the three-point harness and slammed him to the side, wringing a groan from his suddenly compressed lungs.

Rear tires still spinning, the car careened sideways and lifted up on two wheels, threatening to go over sideways. It teetered there for a second before it crashed back to the pavement and shuddered on its tires.

Ty cursed and fought his way out of the harness that had probably saved his life. The driver's door was dented and stuck closed, the window mechanism jammed. Shouting against a slice of pain that ran down the back of his neck all the way to his tailbone, he levered himself around, lifted his legs and kicked out the broken windshield.

It flew free and landed with a crash, and he followed it out and down, hitting the pavement so hard the concussion reverberated through his body, making him fold over and gasp with pain.

When he straightened, he was looking straight up the business end of an M-16 held by a grizzle-cheeked National Guardsman whose bearing shouted ex-combat military. Behind him stood two younger soldiers, with a third fuzz-cheeked Guardsman peering out through the main hatch of the tank.

"You move, I pull the trigger," the veteran said, and there wasn't a hint of maybe in his voice.

Ty's brain raced as he considered and rejected all his possible options. He didn't have time for this. He was still several minutes away from the tunnel, and now he had no wheels.

Not to mention he had maybe eighteen bullets left, compared to the mag of an M-16 in fully automatic mode.

"I'm not moving until you say it's okay," Ty said, holding his hands out at his sides to indicate that he wasn't going for a weapon. "But I'm on your side, buddy. I'm with the feds."

The vet, whose chest tag identified him as Sergeant T. Martin, didn't stand down one inch. "Show me your ID."

"Stolen by a bunch of punk kids," Ty lied. "Along with my badge."

"Then give me your name and who you're with and I'll call it in." Martin sent a sour look at the Camaro. "That isn't an official ride, and even though it got the worst of the crash with my tank, I'm not letting you walk when you've pulled that sort of stunt, after curfew, while packing at least a Glock and a Magnum."

"I don't blame you," Ty said. And then, because lies hadn't been getting him anywhere lately, he said, "Look, if you run my name, you're going to get a hold order and I don't have time for that garbage. I can't tell you the details, but I swear to you that if you don't let me through, a lot of people are going to die."

Martin stiffened imperceptibly, and a muscle ticked at the corner of his jaw. "Sampson and Jimmy, with me. Paulo, you get on the horn and see what the hell is going on." The two soldiers behind the guardsmen moved up to his three and nine, and the third man dropped back through and let the hatch clang shut behind him as the veteran said to Ty, "You're going to need to wait. Hands on your head and turn around."

Ty cursed. "Look, I'm telling the truth here. I'll show you." He faked a reach into his pocket and came up with the revolver, which he cocked and aimed at the leftmost youngster, a smooth-cheeked blond guy whose tag IDed him as S. Sampson.

The three guardsmen froze. Actually, the two kids froze and Martin nearly started shooting, then paused with his finger on the trigger. There was no indecision in his eyes.

No, his look was pure speculation.

Ty risked a breath, knowing he'd guessed right. "I don't want to do this, and you don't want me to. We've both seen too many kids like him die. It doesn't have to happen tonight, Sergeant Martin. Just let me go."

"You're not with the feds," Martin said. "What are you, a merc? You trying to get your hands on a tank? The thing's a piece of junk. Hell, you and your Camaro probably did it a favor, got it that much closer to the scrap heap."

Ty shook his head. "I occasionally do some side work for pay, but I really am a fed. Secret Service, and no, I don't want the damn tank. I want something faster, but just getting the hell out of here will do for now."

"And what happens if I hold you?" Martin asked. "We both know you're not going to cap the kid."

"We both also know you're not going to shoot

me." Ty took a step back. "I've got you wondering, and you're not pulling the trigger until you're sure I'm the enemy."

"Everyone's the enemy in a situation like this," the sergeant replied, raising the weapon an inch, until it was aimed at Ty's left collarbone. "And I'm packing rubber rounds. Probably wouldn't kill you, but it'd sure as hell keep you in one place long enough for Paulo to check your story."

The possibility had Ty freezing in place once again. "Please," he said, his voice cracking on the word. "There's a woman involved."

That same muscle jumped in Martin's jaw. "Your girl?"

"No," Ty said reflexively, then contradicted himself. "Yes."

"Which is it?"

"She's mine." Ty took a deep breath and lowered the revolver, releasing the hammer. "She's mine, damn it, and a bastard named Shea has her. He's going to kill her if I'm not at the Ted Williams in—" he glanced at his watch and the bottom fell out of his world "—four minutes."

Martin let the tip of the M-16 drop an inch. "If that's true, I can have men there in time. We've got a unit right near—"

"That's no good," Ty said. "The guy who has her is calling the shots. He's ex-Special Forces."

"Like you." It wasn't a question.

"I need to get to her," Ty said. "Please."

The sergeant stood for a frozen moment, a teetering second where the balance could've slipped either way. Then he nodded and lowered the M-16. "Go. But if you're screwing with me, I'll hunt you down myself."

"I wouldn't blame you." Ty reholstered the revolver, thought about going back into the Camaro for his knapsack and decided not to bother. "I don't suppose you have a spare jeep on the other side of this piece of garbage?" He knocked on the tank and listened to the echo.

Martin glanced at the Camaro, training his light on the cracked steering column, where wires gaped. "Nope, but I saw a decent looking bike two streets over."

"Thanks." Ty took off at a dead run, hoping like hell he wouldn't be too late, but knowing deep down inside that there was no possible way he could run two blocks, hotwire a motorcycle and make it to the tunnel in time. If only he had—

He skidded to a stop, realizing he'd left his phone in the Camaro, and also realizing it was probably smashed to smithereens.

"Problem?" Martin called.

"Yeah." He thought fast, calculating his odds and finally realizing it was time to call in the cavalry. "Get a message to SAC Epps of the Secret Service. Tell him where I'm going."

Ty knew Epps wasn't the fastest off the mark, and

he was counting on that delay, because he also knew something else.

Ethan had the radio they'd pulled off Ben Parker, an agent who'd been killed by Shea's son Aidan. The message wouldn't just reach SAC Epps.

It'd get to the men of Eclipse, too.

TY'S WATCH SHOWED 5:05, five minutes past Liam's deadline when he hit the entrance to the Ted Williams. The monstrous tunnel had once been a central part of Boston's Big Dig, a huge construction project that had gone five years and several billion dollars beyond initial estimates.

Just before the inauguration, Grant Davis had given a speech at the mouth of the tunnel, promising matching federal funds to help the city and state climb out from underneath the mountain of debt they'd accumulated during the project. Ty knew damn well those funds had been allocated and spent, because the mayor herself had thanked the vice president two days earlier, during cocktails at the John Hancock building.

Right before the lights went out.

His gut knotted tight, he parked the stolen bike and swung down, then crossed a short strip of deserted tarmac to the carved granite ledge where Davis had stood for his speech.

Ty swept his flashlight back and forth over the area,

but there was no sign of Gabby. No Liam. No Grant Davis. Nothing.

On the horizon to the east, visible beyond the flat-lands of Logan Airport, he saw a faint lightening, a hint of pink that separated the sea from the sky. Dawn.

He was too late.

His throat closed on a fist of loss, of failure. Rage flashed through him and he dropped his hands to his guns, ready to draw both of them and shoot.

At what? There was no target. He'd been chasing a ghost, a shadow of a man he'd once known, once respected. A man who'd become—

"You're late," Liam's voice said from behind him.

Adrenaline jolted and Ty cursed and spun, cross-drawing down on the other man in a blink. But he didn't fire. He couldn't.

Liam stood holding Gabby in front of him as a human shield.

"Toss your weapons," Liam ordered.

Relief crashed through Ty. She was alive. *Thank you, God.*

He slid the safeties and tossed both of his guns, but took note of where they landed, just in case he got a chance to go for them. He hoped to hell he'd have a clear shot at Liam if he did, hoped to hell Gabby wouldn't be in the way.

And he prayed he wouldn't be forced to choose between her and the vice president, between her life and a bomb detonating in the city of Boston, because while his career vows and his strategist's training said he'd have to make one decision, his heart said he should make the other.

"I'm here, just like you wanted," he said, shifting on his feet, moving in a wide sweep around Liam's position so the other man was forced to move, forced to stay a little off balance. "What do we do now?"

"We talk," Liam said. In the yellow light from Ty's flashlight and the faint glow from the east, he looked old and tired. "Actually, I talk and you listen."

Come on, Ethan, Ty chanted inwardly, wishing he knew where the other members of Eclipse were, and whether they'd gotten his message.

He had a feeling they hadn't, which left him on his own.

"Gabby," Ty called softly. "Are you okay, sweetheart?" The endearment from their online romance slipped out unexpectedly, but it fit with a solid click beneath his heart, like a lock latching tightly shut around something important.

"I'm not hurt," she said, but even in the wan light he could see the tear tracks on her face and the stark terror in her pale-brown eyes.

"She'll stay that way if you do what I want," Liam said. He jerked his chin into the tunnel. "Let's take a walk. You first."

Covering both Ty and Gabby with his weapon,

Liam marched them into the tunnel. Once they passed inside, he clicked on a high-powered flashlight mounted atop the handgun. His and Ty's flashlights showed a monstrous stone-and-cement arch over four lanes of traffic that were eerily deserted. The arch went only halfway through its semicircle, ending in a center wall that both supported the massive tunnel and separated the inbound and outbound lanes.

Their footsteps echoed hollowly, and the faint light outside faded back to darkness lit only by the flashlight beams, which illuminated circles of stone and pavement and glinted off the luminescent paint that divided the four-lane road.

Ty became aware of the tunnel descending beneath his feet, a subtle downward tilt that riffled the fine hairs on the back of his neck. A snippet of Grant's speech came back to him then in the vice president's powerful, ringing voice. "This massive undertaking tells the story of the great city of Boston," he'd said. "The many miles of tunnel have been hewn out of rock just as the patriots of years gone by struggled to hack freedom from tyranny. The great arch was sunk beneath hundreds of feet of harbor water, set there by engineering feats that trace back to the great architects of colonial times and beyond…. This project represents Boston. It is Boston. And because of that, how can we do anything less than honor it?"

He'd promised federal funds to cover the Big Dig

shortfalls, Ty remembered, and he damn well knew they'd come through. He'd heard the mayor say so himself.

So what did Liam want here? he thought, but as soon as the inner question formed, the answer clicked into being. The bomb.

Liam wasn't trying to kill people. He was trying to make a statement. What better statement than to destroy something his enemy helped create?

"Over there." Liam's light jerked off to the right, toward where a short flight of iron steps led up to a narrow cement catwalk on the short side of the tunnel. "Up the stairs."

Ty followed the instructions, thinking fast as he mounted the steps. The catwalk was just wide enough for a single person, creating a confined area with a wall on one side, a ten-foot drop on the other, and doorways every few hundred yards. If he could somehow signal Gabby to make a dive for it, leaving Liam exposed, he might be able to get the gun, get control of the situation. But how could he signal her?

"Here," Liam said, voice sharp. "Through that door. And don't try anything, or I *will* put a bullet in your girlfriend here."

The professional in Ty said to ignore the dig, but the man in him couldn't. "You hurt her and I'll end you, Liam. That's a promise."

Liam laughed, a dry, derisive bark. "I was ended a

long time ago, Ty, and your friends finished the job when they took out my boys. Now I'm just making sure I take the right people down with me when I go."

Ty took note of a sturdy bar outside the door, one designed to drop into a pair of brand-new hooks, one on either side of the doorway.

They were to be barred in, were they? He'd see about that.

Gritting his teeth, he shoved through the doorway and paused in surprise when he realized he could see. The room was well lit by generator-powered lights, which showed a long, narrow space with an inexplicable maze of pipes and lines and circuit boxes lining the walls. A small pile of camping gear was stacked in one corner, suggesting that Liam had stayed in the room at one time.

A security camera high up on the wall blinked to indicate it was functioning normally, but it had a crude-looking device stuck to its side, with wires running at haphazard angles, suggesting the tape was being looped, or diverted somehow.

Worse, a tall metal cylinder with rounded edges and pressurized spigots at the top sat in a darkened corner formed by a maze of intersecting pipes. It was a pressurized tank of some kind—likely propane, if Liam's second clue was anything to go by. One thing was sure—it didn't belong in the long, narrow room.

Ty cursed low under his breath and crossed to the

tank, one part of him fearing what he'd find, one part of him already knowing.

Sure enough, on the far side of the tank, where the deepest shadows rested, Vice President Grant Davis sat atop a second tank, bound in place with coil after coil of thin wire. His head hung low on his chest. A trickle of blood had dried at his temple and a nasty bruise spread across his cheek, but that wasn't what had Ty sucking in a breath.

Between his feet sat the digital readout for the time-delay detonator Liam had used as his first clue.

As Ty watched, the digital countdown ticked down past the twenty-minute mark.

It was almost dawn.

Chapter Eleven

Gabby, sweetheart, I wish you'd tell me what's going on. I don't understand why we can spend hours trading e-mails and instant messages but we can't meet. You know more about me than just about anybody. Nobody else knows that I'm up most nights because I dream, and I'm betting you don't talk to too many other people about your parents, or about how you'd like to make a change in your life. I bet before we started corresponding, you hadn't even admitted some of those things to yourself. So why can't we set a date? What are you hiding? Are you married? In trouble with the law? An alien in disguise? What? [Sent by TyJ; July 27, 2:30:01 a.m.]

5:20 a.m., August 3
18 Minutes until Sunrise

The moment Gabby had heard Ty's voice outside the tunnel she'd wanted to weep with relief. Just as urgently, she'd wanted to tell him to run, to get away. Liam had passed beyond madness to cold, sociopathic revenge, and he had no intention of letting any of them go free. She was sure of it.

Now, hearing the hollow echo of Ty's curse, she had a feeling he knew it, too.

Liam had explained the setup to her as he'd tied the vice president into place. The main tank contained highly pressurized liquid propane, and the secondary tank Davis sat atop was filled with more of the same. The standard-issue military explosive that sat between Davis's feet—the one Liam had clued them how to circumvent—was merely what Liam had called "crowd control," designed to get and keep Ty's attention.

Liam himself was carrying a remote detonator he could use to blow the tunnel on a moment's notice, using the main device, which was located below them in a narrow access shaft his sons had blocked off, making it nearly impossible to reach. No matter what Ty said or did, the main bomb would detonate at dawn.

They had played Liam's game, but there would be no winners here. Only losers.

"At least let Gabby go," Ty said, his voice quiet and almost pleading. "She's done nothing to you."

Ignoring him, Liam dragged Gabby to the main tank. He forced her arms high over her head and looped the rope binding her wrists over a protrusion higher up, nearly suspending her off the floor. She squirmed and spat and got nowhere.

Once Liam had her arranged to his satisfaction, he turned away, his voice echoing in the small room as he said, "It's down to this, Ty. Only one of us is leaving this room alive. When the time comes, it'll be up to you to choose who it will be. Until then, we're going to have a little chat, and just in case you were thinking of doing something stupid…" There was a pause, and Gabby heard the sound of shifting cloth and motion, and pictured Liam showing Ty the detonator. "No sudden movements."

"Think about this, Liam." Ty's voice was raw with emotion. Having come to know him as well as she did, Gabby could only imagine how hard it was for him to see a former comrade arrive at this point. "You were a good man once, a soldier. This isn't the sort of thing a soldier does to his own people."

"These aren't my people," Liam said. His voice shifted as he moved away a few steps, closer to the vice president. "*He* isn't one of mine." Flesh struck flesh and Davis grunted a curse, the sound nearly drowned out when Liam snarled, "Tell him what you did, Grant. Tell him what sort of man he's been protecting all these years."

Davis groaned but said nothing. There was the sound of another blow, then another. Gabby winced with each punch, though none of them were aimed directly at her. There was pain, though, in her arms and shoulders, and the muscles of her calves, which cramped as she stretched onto her tiptoes in an effort to relieve the strain.

Unable to sustain the stretch, she dropped back flat-footed.

She felt the rope give a fraction.

"Stop it," Ty said in a sharp voice. "Beating some sort of confession out of him means nothing. Sending us across the city chasing our own tails means nothing. Maybe he welched on a few campaign promises. Stuff happens. That doesn't make him responsible for ruining your life. You did that entirely on your own."

Ty's voice moved as he spoke, and Gabby could hear Liam shifting on his feet, facing Ty. At first she didn't understand why Ty was moving, why he was goading the madman holding the detonator.

Then she sagged against her bonds and felt the rope give a little more, and she realized she knew exactly what he was doing.

He was giving her a chance to make a difference.

Come on, Gabby, Ty thought inwardly, willing her to notice that the rope at her wrists was fraying where it was hooked over a sharp-edged metal flange on the propane tank. *Come on, sweetheart, just a little bit more. You can do it.*

Outwardly he fought to keep Liam talking, struggled to keep his focus away from Gabby. "You didn't really expect your little treasure hunt to persuade me, did you? Surely you knew me better than that. I know what I know, and I trust who I trust."

Liam sneered, but at least he'd turned away from Davis, whose head hung even lower now, and whose blood dripped from a split lip to stain his ripped tux shirt. "I remember," Liam said. "You were an idealistic young pup, and you've grown into a blindly loyal dog, haven't you? You're not even willing to look at what's right in front of your face and consider that you might've missed a few things along the way."

The older man held the detonator up and shone his flashlight all along the small unit, admiring it, perhaps, or more likely reminding Ty that he was in control.

Catching a flash of warning on Gabby's face, Ty took a step to the side, angling away from her and forcing Liam to track him as she tugged at the rope. Ty said, "You made a mistake, Liam. You were mad at the insurgents for nearly blowing you away in that car bombing, and you wanted to get yours back. We all knew it. Hell, Commander Bradley made you swear you'd hold it together. You didn't, and innocent people died. That's nobody's fault but your own."

Ty forced himself to focus on Liam, but in his peripheral vision, he could see that Gabby had started working the rope from side to side along the jagged edge of the flange.

Even better, Davis's head had come up, and his swollen eyes were focused on Ty. He gave a brief hand signal, a flick of the wrist in the silent language all three of the men had used so long ago. *Ready when you are.*

He was still bound, but if Gabby could get to him, they might be able to make it three to one, might be able to gain control of the detonator and subdue Liam without bringing the tunnel—and Boston Harbor— down around them.

Maybe.

"It wasn't my fault," Liam insisted, shifting the light so it lit his face. "I swear it on my sons. On my family's honor, I swear I didn't jump the gun on the signal."

"So we're back to the story you told at the trial?" Ty asked, feeling a prickle work its way down his neck when Gabby eased away from the tank and bent to work on Grant's bonds. "You're claiming that Grant set you up by signaling you to cut the power before the commander gave the signal? Then I'll ask you the same question the inquiry board asked before they sent you up for a court martial. Why would he do something like that? You were the one who wanted to get at the insurgents, not him. Davis just wanted to get the hostages out."

"Grant wanted what I had," Liam snarled. "We both had the charisma, but I had the connections and the name. That rescue was going to send us home heroes, and he couldn't bear to let that happen." Before Ty could react, Liam spun to point at Grant Davis. "He—"

The world sped up and everything erupted into a blur of motion and bodies as Grant Davis launched himself at Liam.

"Stay back!" Ty shouted to Gabby, who was inexplicably crumpling toward the ground. Knowing he had to take care of Liam first, he hurled himself into the fray.

He grabbed Liam's left hand, the one holding the detonator, and clamped his fingers around the pressure switch, holding it from popping open and triggering a hell of an explosion. Getting his other arm around Liam's waist, he swung his weight, bringing the three men down in a heap.

"Grab the gun," Ty ordered. "Toss it in the corner."

"Got it," Davis replied, then said something else that wound up lost as Liam exploded beneath his captors. He rammed a bony elbow into Ty's gut, hooked a foot around Ty's leg and heaved himself off the floor with nearly superhuman strength.

"I don't think so." Ty hung on, cursing when fingers pried at his hand, loosening his grip on the detonator. "Grant!" he barked. "Can you get it?"

An elbow connected with Ty's mouth, mashing his teeth against his lips so hard he tasted blood. He spat a curse and fought back, punching and kicking and trying like hell to hold on, though he wasn't entirely sure what body part belonged to whom anymore.

Then his hand was empty. The detonator was gone. In the moment he hesitated over the realization, Liam elbowed him once more and yanked away.

Ty cursed viciously. "Watch it, he's got the—"

A bark of gunfire cut him off, and the man beneath him shuddered and went limp.

"Grant!" Horror slashed through Ty—the failure of losing a protectee, losing a friend. "No!"

He grabbed for the limp figure and took a quick inventory of the wound. He was so focused on the injury it took him a moment to realize that the mortally wounded man wasn't Grant Davis.

It was Liam.

A bright red bloom spread across his chest and his eyes rolled white and scared. His mouth pulled tight in a rictus of pain, of disbelief, and he reached for Ty.

Ty turned toward the door. "Grant, thank God. Do you have the detonator?"

Davis stood partway across the room, battered and bloodied, holding Liam's gun in one hand and the detonator in the other. Something hard and cold and unfamiliar moved through his expression. "Yeah, I do."

He dropped the small unit and ground it underfoot.

"No!" Ty grabbed for the thing, but it was too late. Furious, he snapped, "Grant, for chrissake, we could've used that to help disarm the main device!"

The vice president nodded. "I know, and I'm sorry. But I have a reputation to protect."

Without another word he slipped through the door, which shut with a thunk.

Ty shouted and flung himself at the door, but he was too late. Grant had dropped the welded bar into place.

"Damn it!" Ty jammed his shoulder against the panel, cursing when it didn't budge.

Pulse riding high, he spun and crossed to the propane tanks. He crouched down to Gabby, realizing that Grant must've cold-cocked her.

"Gabby? Sweetheart, are you hurt?" He got no response, and her muscles were lax under his hand when he touched her shoulder. New panic spurted. "Gabby!"

His shout echoed in the small space and his heart clutched in his chest when she didn't respond.

Then he saw her throat move, and heard her faint moan.

"Gabby." He bent close and touched his lips to her cheek, ran his hands over her, gently trying not to move her if she was seriously hurt.

He found a raised knot at the back of her head, and hot anger flared. Grant Davis had done this. The man he'd trusted. The man he'd defended. The man he'd vowed to take a bullet for.

Right now he'd rather put a bullet *in* the bastard.

"I'm okay. I'm fine." Gabby roused finally, pulling herself up to a sitting position and batting at his hands, but then she sank against him, tucking her head beneath his jaw. "Ow. I didn't see that one coming."

"Me, neither," Ty said. "I'm sorry. I should've listened to you instead of being stubborn."

But there was no time for more explanations or comfort. The display showed eleven minutes until sunrise, until detonation.

Ty helped Gabby to her feet and propped her against the wall when she swayed. Then he knelt down beside the man he'd once called a teammate, once called a traitor.

Liam looked like an old man now. An old, dying man. The lines across his forehead and beside his mouth cut deep grooves, his eyes were closed and his skin had gone waxy pale. His shirt was soaked with dark blood, but none appeared to be flowing bright red from the bullet Davis had put in his chest.

For a second Ty thought Liam was already gone. Then he stirred and opened his eyes. Lifting a trembling, bloodstained hand, he gripped Ty's wrist with surprising strength. His lips moved, forming words without sound. "I'm sorry."

At another time, under other circumstances and with a different man, it would have been a time for absolution. But with the seconds and minutes ticking down, there was no time for niceties. Ty leaned in, grabbed Liam's shirt and twisted it in his fist for leverage so he could lift the wounded man partway up and get in his face. "Where's the access point and what's the code to disarm the countdown?"

Liam's eyes locked on his, and Ty could see failure and regret, could hear both in the other man's voice when he said, "The bastard won, didn't he?"

It was true. Grant Davis had, in one cold, calculated motion, gotten rid of the three people who knew his secret. By his actions, he'd admitted the truth of Liam's accusation. He'd ruined a good man to forward his own political career. Now he'd add three lives to the tally on his soul, but that last glimpse Ty had gotten of Grant's eyes had told the full story.

Grant didn't care. As far as he was concerned, three lives were nothing compared to the lure of the main stage at the White House.

Burning anger flared in Ty's gut. "Not if I have anything to say about it, he hasn't. But I need your help. Give me the disarming code, and Gabby and I will make sure everyone knows what kind of man he really is."

He didn't say he'd get Liam out safely because they both knew Liam was clinging to life only through sheer stubbornness. He wouldn't leave the tunnel alive.

His fingers tightened on Ty's wrist, grinding down to bone. "Swear it. Promise me you'll make sure he doesn't become president."

Something shifted inside Ty, something hard and sure. The realization that in the end, despite the differences in their methods and histories, he and Liam were very alike. He growled, "I swear if we get out of here, Grant Davis is finished in politics."

Liam locked eyes with him for a long moment, then nodded. The air seemed to drain out of him and his voice grew weak as he said, "The access hatch is behind the secondary tank. There's no disarm code. It's standard configuration. You won't have any problem with it."

Those last few words, almost whispered, confirmed what Ty had begun to suspect.

Liam Sullivan hadn't ever intended to kill Davis. He'd wanted an eye for an eye, a reputation for a reputation, and this elaborately planned blackout had been the only way he could conceive to make people listen to him. That didn't make it right, and it didn't make him sane, but it did make Ty think the wrong man was leaking his life away right now.

What would have happened if things had gone differently eleven years earlier? He didn't know, but he had a feeling a number of lives would be different now. Including his.

And Gabby's.

He glanced at her now, and his heart clutched a little in his chest. She looked so beautiful, so fragile. He wanted to hold her, to comfort her while the world went on around them.

Instead it was up to him to make sure their worlds continued at all.

"Thank you." He gripped Liam's shoulder briefly,

then gestured to Gabby. "Sit with him while I crawl down and disarm the main device in—" he glanced at the display "—eight minutes or less."

He stood, trying to find the strange calm that had once steadied him through the hairiest situations, when his assignments had ranged from defusing homemade land mines in the Middle East to precision detonations that could vaporize a single restaurant table while leaving its neighbors untouched.

Once, that calm had been second nature. Now it eluded him, losing to a tight fear that centered on the woman standing opposite him, the one he paused in front of. He stood there for half a second, wanting to tell her something, wanting to promise her something, but unable to find the words.

In the end he simply leaned down and kissed her. "See you soon."

As she crouched down beside Liam, murmuring softly, Ty shoved some of the camping gear aside to reveal the access hatch. In the dim light, it took a moment for his brain to process the sight of a metal bar bolted across the hatch at an angle. When he did, his curse was low and bitter. There was no way he was getting through the narrow space that remained.

"What's wrong?" Gabby said quickly.

"They've blocked the hatch. It'll open because it swings in, but I won't be able to fit through. No way in hell." Ty dropped back down beside Liam. His eyes were closed, his breathing shallow, but Ty spared the dying man little pity in shaking him awake. "It's blocked," he snapped the moment Liam's eyelids fluttered open. "I need another access point."

Liam's expression clouded, then went sad. "Aidan. He told the others I wouldn't go through with it. He was the one who wanted to block the opening."

"Well, he did. What's your backup?"

"There isn't one." Liam shook his head, his eyes full of grief and regret. "We welded the other hatches shut from the inside."

It hit Ty then that this could be it. The end. With no way out of the little room and no way to get to the bomb, there seemed like nothing left to do but say goodbye to the people he loved.

At the thought he looked for Gabby, only to find her crouched down by the hatch, feeling the edges of the opening.

When he knelt down beside her and took her hand, she turned to him, face set with determination. "I can make it through."

He squeezed her hand. "Maybe. But they've welded the other exits. There's no way out."

"I'm not talking about escaping." She turned her beautiful, sightless eyes to him. "If I can get through there, can you walk me through defusing the bomb?"

Chapter Twelve

Dearest Ty:

I'm not married or in jail, but that doesn't change the fact that I can't take what we have into face-to-face reality. Because of that, and because what we have now doesn't seem to be enough for you, though it's everything to me, I think it'd be best for us to stop corresponding. Which is another first for me. I've never fallen for a guy online, never fought with a guy online, and I've never broken up with a guy before, online or in person. It's always been the other way around. So thank you for that, my special friend. Thank you for so many firsts even though in the end, they weren't enough. With love, Gabriella.
[Sent by CyberGabby; July 28, 3:38:08 a.m.]

5:33 a.m., August 3
5 Minutes until Dawn

Gabby didn't wait for Ty to argue or tell her she couldn't do it. She shucked out of his windbreaker and tossed it aside, figuring it would be more hindrance than protection where she was going. Then she tucked in her shirt. Scant preparations, perhaps, but there was neither time nor resources for more. "What am I going to need down there?" she asked, willing him to trust her, to believe that she was challenged but not handicapped.

And in willing it, she realized that she really believed it now, for the first time ever.

She was blind, not incapacitated. Ty couldn't get through the blocked hatch but she could. She couldn't see what she would be working on, but he could help with that.

For now, at least, they could fill the gaps in each other.

He'd been silent for so long she thought he was going to waste precious time arguing. Instead, as she reached for the hatch once more, he slid an arm around her waist and hitched her up so they were chest to chest, breathing the same air.

"Gabby," he said, pressing a small pair of pliers into her hand. "You can do this. I trust you. I believe in you. I think… God, I think I'm falling in love with you. I think I fell months ago, when I was pretending to be somebody else who was really me."

His words hung in the air, heavy with meaning, with desperation. She could feel the pound of his heart and the rasp of his indrawn breaths, and for the first time since she'd stepped out into the courtyard to rescue Maria from a madman with a gun, she felt like she knew this man, had known him for months, maybe had always known him.

"Ty," she said, forming the single syllable with her tongue as she had done so many nights, sitting at her keyboard, chatting with the man she'd come to know and love and depend on. Even though neither of them had been truthful, they'd both shown their true selves. "I feel the same way." She took a deep breath. "I think I'm in love with you, too."

Despite it all, CyberGabby had fallen for the real Ty Jones and TyJ had fallen for the real Gabby Solaro.

Exultation thrilled through her, hot and hard, and for a moment she felt as though she was back in the Camaro, flying through the night with the wind in her hair. Carrying that joy, that adventure, she leaned in and touched her lips to his.

There was nothing tentative or questioning in this kiss; it was all raw power and demand, all tooth and tongue and the edgy sensuality she'd thought was gone for good. Only, now she realized it had been waiting for her to grow up, for her to grow out of her shell and come back to life.

He said her name again and she said his, and there was nothing left to say. There was only another kiss, a soft promise that there would be more to come later. After.

Then she drew away from him, tucked the pliers in her back pocket and felt her way to the access hatch.

The mechanism gave easily beneath her touch and the panel dropped inward on well-oiled hinges.

Gabby took a deep breath and said to herself as much as Ty, "I can do this."

"*We* can do this." There was no question in his words, only a quiet confidence she took with her as she wiggled her way between the sharp metal slat and the edge of the hatch, and dropped face-first into a rectangular shaft that sloped gently downward.

She wrinkled her nose against the smell of dust and oil, and used her hands to worm along until her feet passed through the hatch, and she was able to belly-crawl faster. Feeling the walls of the narrow chute closing in on her, she called, "How far does this tunnel go?"

The shout echoed in the small space, making her already-sore head pound harder, but there was no time for that pain. Not now, when the seconds were ticking down beneath her skin.

"You haven't reached the end yet?" Ty's voice was distorted and strange, making her feel very alone all of a sudden.

"Not yet… Wait," she called, cranking her voice for the added confidence it gave her, despite the echoes. She felt the edge of the shaft, felt only nothingness beyond. "I've got it. I'm going in."

Before Ty could object, she gripped the slightly protruding edge and used the handhold to work her body and legs out of the chute. The muscles in her upper arms burned with fatigue and strain as she lowered herself, and panic spurted when she couldn't find the floor with her feet.

The echo patterns told her it was a small room, probably eight-by-ten, with irregular walls, a ceiling and a floor. But she couldn't see the floor, couldn't be sure it was really there.

"Believe it, Gabby," she told herself. Squeezing her eyelids tightly shut as visions of elevator shafts flashed in her mind's eye, she let go of her handhold and jumped.

The drop was maybe two feet, but it was the longest two feet of her life. The impact jarred her and she fell to her knees, but she'd never been so glad before to skin her palms on a concrete floor.

She stood and turned to the shaft, calling, "I'm in. I'm okay. What do I do?"

"First, find the wires that lead down the shaft."

She traced her way back up the wall, wincing when her fingers trailed across something faintly moist and slimy, then uttered a low cry when she reached the trailing wires. "I've got them."

"Good. Follow them to the primary device. It looks like—" He broke off, then corrected himself. "It'll feel like a flat, smooth box that's rounded on the edges. There'll be a couple of knobs on one side. The wires you already found should enter the box on the other side."

"Am I going to kill us if I touch the wrong thing?" she called, swallowing around a mass of sick nerves.

"Not yet."

"That wasn't exactly reassuring."

"Wasn't meant to be. You have the box?"

Her fingers glanced off a smooth surface that was oddly warm to the touch, as though the detonator was alive. "Yes. I've got it."

"Okay, here's what you're going to do…" As he walked her through the procedure step by step, she un-latched the housing and bared the guts of the detonator, working by feel and trying not to let her hands shake.

"How much time do we have left?" she asked when he paused.

"Enough. Now, we're down to the last step, and this is where it gets really tough." Ty's voice went ragged. "You're going to feel three wires leading from the timer to the charge. One's hot, one's cold, one's neutral. I need you to cut the cold. You cut the hot and it blows. You cut the neutral and it does nothing."

"How do I know which one is cold?"

"It's black."

"Oh." Sick fear rolled through Gabby, stealing her breath and making her head spin. A bead of sweat formed on her brow and itched, but she didn't dare take her hand off the wires to brush it away.

Tracing the outline of the detonator with her fingers, she called, "I feel three wires coming out of a small rectangular box, maybe the size of my hand. There's a wire on the left, one on the right and one in the middle. Does that help?"

"There's no way to tell which way he put it in," Ty said hollowly. "And there's no way to ask him. He's dead."

Gabby took a deep breath. "Then guess. If Liam put this thing together, how would he have done it? Isn't there a standard way of doing it or something?"

There was a pause, then Ty said. "There's a military SOP, but…"

"But what?"

"I always did it the other way around. Liam knew that. If he was putting this together for me, he might've done it that way."

Gabby heard the corollary in the silence. *Or he might not have.*

"You knew him," she said. "He trusted you to see the truth when everyone else around you refused. What do you think he did?"

She knew it wasn't fair to put it all on him. She could picture the war going on inside his psyche, where what logic told him wasn't always what his heart believed.

The seconds bled away. Her heart pushed up into her throat and lodged there, choking her breath to a thin stream of oxygen. "Ty?"

"Cut the one on the left," he said finally.

She wanted to ask if he was sure, but didn't because she already knew the answer. He was guessing, flying blind. They both were.

"Left it is," she said as much to herself as to him, and lifted the needle-nosed pliers into place, working them until the thin wire was poised between the sharpened edges at the back of the tool.

Gabby paused and took a breath.

And cut the wire.

The device gave off a screeching beep that raised the hairs on the back of her neck and had her bracing for all hell to break loose.

Nothing happened.

Out in the main room, the alarm on Ty's watch went off, signaling the dawn.

Gabby exhaled with a whoosh that turned to a whoop, one that was echoed in Ty's deeper tones. Heart pounding, excitement hammering through her veins, she dropped the pliers and flung herself toward the narrow shaft, scrambling up and into it and worming her way back up to the main room, back up to the man who waited for her, the man who'd come through for her, just like he'd promised.

"We did it!" she crowed when she felt the edges of the hatch beneath her fingertips. She reached through the narrow opening to link fingers with Ty.

"*You* did it," he corrected, and pulled her through, pulled her into his arms. "You were so brave."

"I was petrified." She nuzzled against him, needing his warmth and strength. With the danger past and adrenaline fading, she began to shake as reality caught up with her and she comprehended what could have happened to them. What nearly *had* happened to them.

"We could've died." Her words came out muffled as she pressed her face against his throat, his jaw, any part of him she could reach.

"We didn't." He caught her lips with his, and his kiss tasted of survival, of life. "Thanks to you."

Heat flared and she rose up on her tiptoes to wrap her arms around his neck and give herself to the moment, to the man. Where before she'd been afraid of the flare of power, scared of the mad impulses that rocketed through her body, now she gloried in them.

The kiss spun out in a mad promise of things to come, broken only when a loud clanging sounded at the door, along with the muffled sounds of men's voices.

Gabby drew away from Ty but put her hand in his, turning to face the door as it flung open and the voices came clear.

For a moment nobody spoke. Then Ty said, "What the hell took you so long?"

Gabby heard three sets of footsteps, three new voices that sorted themselves into individuals as Ty introduced them. "Gabby, I'd like you to meet Ethan, Chase and Shane." He paused, and she felt something shift between them when he said, "The four of us are part of an off-the-books black ops team called Eclipse. We're the guys the Pentagon calls when the regular military can't get it done."

Then he slid a possessive arm around her waist and touched his lips to her cheek. "Only this time, *you* were the one who got it done when we couldn't."

THE NEXT FEW MINUTES were utter chaos as SAC Epps and a combined task force arrived en masse, five minutes too late as usual.

Ty was more than happy to let the other agent take over the scene. He urged Gabby out of the room that had nearly become their tomb. Men and vehicles crowded the tunnel outside the maintenance room, crisscrossing the four-lane roadway in crazy patterns of headlight and flashlight beams.

Ethan, Shane and Chase followed them, and the four members of Eclipse, along with Gabby, formed a loose knot out in the roadway, talking over the situation in low tones.

"Liam was right," Ty said, knowing it would take time for it to sink in, for all the pieces to rearrange themselves in his head. "Grant really did set him up. Hell, for all we know, he wouldn't have carried Liam out of the building if Bradley hadn't stumbled on them."

"We'll take care of it," Ethan said simply. He gripped Ty's shoulder and nodded. "We'll make sure things are set as right as they can be."

Ty nodded. "Mission accomplished, then, albeit with some mop-up work left to do."

Normally after an op, the teammates might have gone out and gotten drunk together, picked a fight together, but Ty had a strong feeling all that was going to change.

Liam had changed each of them, inadvertently making them better.

Ty couldn't help thinking of how happy Ethan had looked the night before, reunited with Rebecca and their son Jesse. Shane and Chase had also found the missing pieces of themselves over the past two days. Shane had fallen hard for Princess Ariana LeBron, and Chase had been reunited with Lily Garrett just in time to meet the newborn daughter he'd known nothing about.

Each of them had grown stronger and gotten better, because of Liam's revenge.

At the thought, Ty glanced down at his hand, which was still joined with Gabby's, then up to her face, which was tipped up to his in inquiry, as if she, too, was wondering where they were supposed to go from there.

He couldn't believe he'd fallen so hard so fast, but he supposed it wasn't really that fast. They'd been working up to it for more than five months. Some of what each of them had written might have been lies, but the emotions had been true.

"Gabby," he began, turning to face her. "I—"

"Jones!" SAC Epps barked. He strode out of the

small maintenance room, jogged down the stairs and joined the group in the road.

Epps scowled at Ty, but then shot an uneasy look that included Shane, Chase and Ethan. The four members of Eclipse formed an imposing unit, and Ty was aware that they were the subject of several rumors more or less based on fact.

No doubt that was why Epps's voice bordered on conciliatory when he said, "Glad you're alive. We'll talk about you shooting Ledbetter after you've been debriefed. Nice job getting Patriot away from that bastard alive."

Once, that had been Ty's only goal. Now he growled, "Do you have him secured?"

Epps's scowl deepened. "Of course. We got your message and arrived to find him trying to get a motorcycle started outside the tunnel. He put up a bit of a fight, tried to get away. Must've gotten confused and thought we were working with that guy back there." He jerked a thumb over his shoulder.

Ty tensed, but he knew now wasn't the time to defend Liam or defame the vice president.

The time for that would come later, but he damn well intended to fulfill his promise.

Grant Davis was done in politics, starting now, and if Ty had anything to say about it, he'd be doing some time behind bars, as well.

"Miss…Solaro, is it?" Epps said, switching his

scowl in her direction. "I have agents waiting to escort you home so you can get cleaned up and change. After that, Agent Wilder will escort you to our field office for debriefing."

"You keep Wilder." Ty stepped partway in front of Gabby. "I'll be in charge of escorting Miss Solaro, and I'll damn well sit in on her debriefing. Just try and stop me."

But Ethan touched Ty's arm, pulled him aside and said under his breath, "We're supposed to be wheels-up within the hour. Dana's going over Epps's head to get you cleared from the debriefing. We're headed to the desert, back to those caves we hit a few months ago. The rebels killed a family at the embassy, then took hostages. Dana says it's bad."

And if Eclipse's seen-it-all Pentagon contact said it was bad, then it was *bad*.

Ty's gut knotted and he glanced back over to Gabby, only to find her watching him, her expression unreadable. He said to Ethan, "I don't think I should—"

"Go," she said firmly, loudly enough to bring Epps's head up. "I'll be fine."

Ty shook his head and grimaced at Ethan. "No. I can't. I need to start making different choices, beginning now. Gabby needs me. I'm staying."

"Excuse us." Gabby took his arm and pulled him aside, gesturing for him to find someplace private. When they'd reached the edge of the gathered rescue vehicles and stopped, Gabby turned to face him, her expression pensive.

"Don't worry," he said before she could speak. "I'll tell them I can't go, that you need me here to go over what happened with Liam and Grant Davis. You won't have to go through this alone."

Instead of looking relieved, she shook her head. "Let it go, Tyler. I'm not Mandy."

The name hit him like a fist to the throat, followed by a punch of anger. He lowered his voice. "I never thought you were."

"But that's how you're acting," she countered. "If you'd stayed home that night, you might've been able to get her to the hospital in time. Maybe. But you weren't and she didn't, and that's the awful truth." She shook her head, seeming to withdraw behind an invisible barrier separating them. "But it doesn't mean you need to stay for me."

"It's not a problem." He took her hands in his and stroked his thumb across one of her wrists, trying to soothe her. "I'll stay."

She looked at him for a long moment before she said. "I'm not asking you to stay." She paused. "In fact, I'm telling you to go. Please. Just go."

The world went still around him. Sound and motion and touch ceased to exist as he waited for her to take the words back, to say she hadn't meant them. But just like that final goodbye e-mail, when she'd said they wanted very different things, her words now held the ring of certainty, of immovable, granite belief.

"Go," she said softly. "I'll be fine without you. I promise."

After a long, shuddering moment, he did exactly that. He turned away and left her standing at the end of the action.

He turned back. "Gabby?"

She only smiled and stood there as though the past six hours hadn't meant anything to her.

As he watched, rosy light spilled through the far end of the tunnel, silhouetting her against the dawn. It was the beginning of a new day.

And, apparently, the end of something wonderful that never had a chance.

Chapter Thirteen

Gabby sweetheart, I know you think this can't possibly work and we should just call it quits. So, logically, what's the downside to meeting in person? I'm in Boston for the night and the Big Guy's meetings were canceled because of the blackout. Meet me at ten o'clock tonight. Please. Anywhere. You pick it and I'll be there, even if I have to fight the entire National Guard to reach you.
Love, Ty.
[Sent by TyJ; Aug 2, 8:30:07 p.m.]

9:55 p.m., August 20

Ty stood in the shadows outside Zia Maria's, a small restaurant in Boston's North End, wishing like hell he were somewhere else.

Strategically placed floodlights broke the darkness and lit Hanover Street, casting warm shadows for pedestrians to pass through as they walked in the balmy summer air. Nearby, a couple walked hand in hand, the woman tipping her head against the man's shoulder as he laughed aloud.

The scene and setting should have been almost painfully romantic. Instead, it gathered a hard knot of nerves in Ty's gut. He hated the idea of meeting the others here, in the restaurant run by Gabby's best friend, when things remained so unsettled between them. But it had been Ethan's call, Ethan's invitation, a command performance for the members of Eclipse and their new families to meet in person for the first time since the blackout.

Ty didn't know how Ethan had come to choose Zia Maria's. Ethan had ducked the question when asked, but he'd made it clear the dinner was nonnegotiable. There was business to discuss, he'd said. Serious business.

So Ty had finished up another round of interviews with the task force investigating the now ex-vice president's improprieties and drove up from D.C., his emotions in turmoil. He was in Gabby's hometown, no more than a few blocks away from her apartment, but he wasn't even sure he was going to see her.

She'd been evasive, refusing to commit to a meeting via e-mail or phone, dodging each time he'd pressed, just as she'd been doing in the weeks since he'd taken off for the Middle East, leaving her to handle the Grant Davis fallout on her own.

She'd told him, repeatedly, that she hadn't minded, but if that were the case, why wouldn't she see him?

"You going to stand out here all night?" a familiar voice said from behind Ty, interrupting his thoughts.

He turned and forced an easy grin. "Hey, Chase. I was just checking out the menu." Ignoring his teammate's snort, he nodded to the petite woman at Chase's side, who had a profusion of red curls sprouting from her head—Little Orphan Annie all grown up and turned into a tiny dynamo of a bombshell. An even tinier bombshell rested in the crook of her arm, looking like a feminized version of Chase, but with her mother's snub nose and devilish smile. "You'd be Lily, then. Congratulations on the engagement. And the little one, of course."

Lily leaned into her fiancé with a secretive, satisfied smile and offered her hand. "It's a pleasure to meet you, Ty. I've heard a great deal about you."

Ty mocked a groan. "I can only imagine." He waved toward the restaurant. "Shall we?"

The others were waiting inside—Shane with Princess Ariana, Ethan with his wife, Rebecca, and their son, Jesse, all apparently recovered from the harrowing experience Liam and his sons had put them through. Ty nodded and smiled and joked with his teammates, keeping up a front of normalcy, while his insides churned. He should've gone to Gabby's house and pounded on the door until she let him in, despite what she'd said. She should be here with him right now, at his side, forming a unit, a couple.

But she'd said that even though she loved him, she wasn't ready for that. He feared she'd meant *he* wasn't ready, but he was. Mandy had been gone nearly eight years, and it was time for him to start living again, to start loving again.

If only he could get Gabby to sit down and talk to him long enough to make her believe.

"What do you think, Ty?" Ethan said.

When he looked up and found the others staring at him expectantly, he shook his head. "I'm sorry, I was—" He broke off. What exactly was he doing? This was ridiculous. He pushed his drink aside and stood. "I'm going to step out for a minute. There's something I have to take care of."

"Sit," Ethan waved him back. "We need you for a vote. I want to add a new member to the group."

"What?" Ty dropped back into his chair without thinking, not sure which part surprised him the most— that Ethan was actually talking about adding a fifth member to Eclipse, or that they were discussing it over breadsticks in an Italian restaurant, with their significant others present.

Then again, he supposed, each of them had been touched by what it meant to be a member of Eclipse— the danger of it, the excitement—and had been forced to acknowledge what those things could mean to the women in their lives.

To Ty that had been a hell of a lesson, which was

why he said, "Actually, you may not want me voting on this one. I've been thinking of retiring."

"Of course we want you to vote," Ethan said as though he hadn't heard the *R* word. "But I want everyone to get a chance to meet her first."

"Her?" Ty frowned. "You're bringing Dana into the field? I know we talked about it before, but—" He broke off as the door swung inward and a knockout walked into Zia Maria's.

Her fiery chestnut hair was cut in a sassy bob that swung near her shoulders and sent the natural waves into an energetic halo. Deft makeup accented her high-boned cheeks and full lips, and dusky rose-colored sunglasses perched on her nose, even though it was nighttime. Her killer curves shouted from inside a pair of low-cut jeans and a soft suede jacket, with a glimpse of firm stomach showing when she turned and said something to the olive-skinned young Romeo manning the front. The maître d' tipped back his head and laughed outright before turning and gesturing to the table where Ty and the others waited.

The knockout turned and strode across the restaurant with a loose, confident stride that added a sexy wiggle to the whole package. It took Ty a moment to notice the pitch-black German shepherd at her side. The glossy-coated animal strode with equally loose strides, its triangular ears pricked and a look of intense concentration on its canine face.

Gabby. Ty didn't say her name out loud—at least he didn't think he had—but she came directly to him, her expression lighting with pleasure, and a glint of the devil.

"Hello, Ty." She touched his arm lightly, orienting herself, and leaned up on tiptoe to brush her lips against his cheek. "Surprise." Then she smiled at the others. "Everyone else here?"

"Waiting on you." With Ty frozen in place, Ethan rose and pulled out a chair for Gabby, then made a round of introductions that made it clear this wasn't the first time she'd met the women. Gabby and Rebecca seemed particularly tight, with Gabby winking at the other woman. "Thanks for recommending that salon on Newbury Street." She touched her hair lightly. "I was ready for a change."

"Apparently more than one." Ty shook his head, trying to clear it. When that didn't work he said, "Gabby? What's going on here?" He looked around the table. "Chase? Shane? You knew about this?"

She took his hand and tugged him down to his chair after making sure her guide dog was safely off to one side. "Don't be mad, Ty. I swore them to silence. I wanted—" she broke off and corrected herself "—I *needed* to get to this point by myself. I had to find a happy medium between the teenage terror I'd been and the insecure woman I'd become. I couldn't let you do that for me. I needed the space to figure it out on my own."

Ignoring the others, and the sight of Maria's dark

head peeking out from around the kitchen door as she blatantly eavesdropped, Ty said, "Then you weren't mad that I left?"

She laughed. "Mad? As I remember it, I practically had to load you on the plane myself." Leaning in, she framed his face in her hands. "I don't want you to take care of me. I want you to share things with me. I want us to back each other up."

"Please tell me you're not talking about working in the field." The thing was, he could almost see it, and the idea sent a chill of fear, a thrill of excitement through him.

"Not exactly." She flexed her fingers onto an imaginary keyboard and pantomimed typing. "I'm going to be your computer backup. I can run searches with the best of them, and, as you can attest, I can hack into just about any database there is. Which is what got me into this mess in the first place." But her tone was light, teasing, inviting him to join in on the fun. "I might even work with Shane to design a few gadgets for his security company."

"That's..." Perfect, Ty realized. She'd be exactly the sort of centralized info-gatherer they'd needed more than a few times on assignment, and from the new sparkle in her eye, she'd found just the adventure she'd been looking for. But where did that leave them?

"I vote in favor of the new member," he said, standing and reaching a hand down for Gabby. "And now we're leaving."

Ignoring Ethan's blatant grin, Ty hustled Gabby out of the restaurant, doing his damnedest not to get tangled in the leash when her startled dog leaped up and tried to guide her, only to find Ty in the way. He was close to cursing by the time he got her outside, into the dark of night. He turned and marched them down the street nearly a block before he stopped and turned to her. "Why didn't you tell me you'd been talking to Ethan about working for Eclipse?" He paused. "Strike that. Why have you been avoiding me?"

For the first time since she'd walked in the restaurant door, her new gleam of confidence faltered. She dropped a hand to trail her fingertips over the dog's head. "I needed to figure out who I am, Ty. I couldn't do that with you around. You would've tried to fix too many things for me. I had to do it myself."

"And now?"

She lifted her hand, touched her new haircut and smiled a soft, feminine smile. "I'm getting there. I like myself. I like the direction I'm headed." She took a deep breath. "If we were still just online friends, I'd be ready to meet you in person. As it is, I'm ready to…" She trailed off, fidgeted with her hair and finally let her hand drop, so she was standing open and accessible. "Did you mean what you said back in the tunnel? More important, do you still feel that way?"

The sudden flare of nerves in her pale eyes gave him all the answer he needed. All the confidence in the world, and the belief that this time he wouldn't mess it up. He was different now. She was different.

Together, they were different.

He took a single step, closing the gap between them as pedestrians strolling Hanover Street eddied around them. "Are you asking if I still love you? How about you tell me first?"

She took a deep breath, caught her full lower lip between her teeth and then whispered, "I love you, Ty Jones."

Those five small but so important words unfurled hope within him. Joy bloomed. Relief.

Love.

He dropped his forehead to touch hers and exhaled. "I love you back, Gabriella Solaro. We may have gotten here in a pretty unorthodox way, but I promise you I'll do everything in my power to get it right from here on out. No more tricks, no more lies."

She laughed and leaned into him. "I think that's something we can both promise."

He eased in for a kiss, and the hard, hurting ball that'd been lodged in his chest for the past few weeks dissolved in a rush of warmth and anticipation. Not caring that they were in the middle of the sidewalk, he wrapped his arms around her and held her as tightly as he could, as tightly as he dared, then tighter still as he kissed her again.

The dog barked and nudged him, and Gabby pulled away to laugh. "This is Fawn, by the way."

"Nice to meet you, Fawn. Let's go for a ride." He held his hand down for the guide dog to sniff, then took Gabby's arm and urged her across the sidewalk. He guided Gabby to the vehicle he'd meter-parked a block down from Zia Maria's.

When Gabby felt the edge of the T-top, she threw her head back and laughed aloud. "You didn't!"

"I sure did." He slid an arm around her waist and lowered his voice to a growl. "I promise we can go as fast as you like, and then some."

She leaned into him, looked up at him with a devilish light in her eyes. "Does this mean you're glad I finally agreed to meet you in person?"

"It means I don't intend to ever let you go again," he said, suddenly serious. "And I want you to promise me something. I'm going to quit the Secret Service and do something that requires less travel. I can work with Shane, maybe, or Ethan. But if I'm staying with Eclipse, jobs are going to come up on short notice. I need you to promise me that you'll tell me if you need me to stay home. Ever."

She closed her eyes for a moment, then nodded. "I promise." When she opened her eyes again, he saw love, and trust. She tapped her palm against the top of the Camaro. "How much time and gas do you have?"

"As much as you need," he said. "You want to go to California? I'm game."

"Close," she said, smiling as a new sort of peace washed across her expression. "I want to go to Miami.

I want to see my parents and Amy. If nothing else, I want them to know I understand now. They didn't shut me out because I was a bad kid, or because they blamed me for being blind. They stepped back because they didn't know how to get over feeling guilty." She touched her lips to the hollow beneath his jaw. "You taught me that."

He returned the kiss. "And you taught me how to let go of things that are long past. Thank you."

She smiled. "Thank you right back." Then she opened the passenger door, urged Fawn into the small back seat and slid onto the black leather seat, looking as if she'd been born to go fast. "Let's ride."

As Ty rounded the car, he glanced back at the restaurant to see a knot of people gathered on the sidewalk, watching with undisguised curiosity. He laughed and waved to them, to his oddly matched family that formed such a perfect unit, made stronger by the women and children who'd been so recently added, who wouldn't have been there if it hadn't been for Liam. His revenge had given each of them a family.

And maybe, in the end, that wasn't such a bad legacy to leave behind.

* * * * *

Look for Jessica Andersen's next
Harlequin Intrigue when
DOCTOR'S ORDERS *comes out*
in January 2008!

Bailey DelMonico has finally
gotten her life on track, and is
passionate about her recent career
change. Nothing will stand in the way
of her becoming a doctor...that is,
until she's paired with the sharp-tongued
Dr. Ivan Munro.

Watch the sparks fly in

Doctor in the House

by *USA TODAY* Bestselling Author

Marie Ferrarella

Available September 2007

Intrigued? Read more at
TheNextNovel.com

nocturne™

Look for

NIGHT MISCHIEF

by

NINA BRUHNS

Lady Dawn Maybank's worst nightmare
is realized when she accidentally conjures
a demon of vengeance, Galen McManus. What
she doesn't realize is that Galen plans to teach
her a lesson in love—one she'll never forget....

DARK
ENCHANTMENTS

Available October wherever you buy books.

*Don't miss the last installment of Dark Enchantments,
SAVING DESTINY by Pat White, available November.*

Silhouette®

Romantic
SUSPENSE

Sparked by Danger,
Fueled by Passion.

When evidence is found that Mallory Dawes
intends to sell the personal financial information
of government employees to "the Russian,"
OMEGA engages undercover agent Cutter Smith.
Tailing her all the way to France, Cutter is
fighting a growing attraction to Mallory while at
the same time having to determine her connection
to "the Russian." Is Mallory really the mouse in
this game of cat and mouse?

Look for
Stranded with a Spy

by *USA TODAY* bestselling author
Merline Lovelace
October 2007.

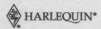

HARLEQUIN®

Mediterranean NIGHTS™

*Sail aboard the luxurious Alexandra's Dream and
experience glamour, romance, mystery and revenge!*

Coming in October 2007...

AN AFFAIR TO REMEMBER

by

Karen Kendall

When Captain Nikolas Pappas first fell in love with
Helena Stamos, he was a penniless deckhand and she
was the daughter of a shipping magnate. But he's
never forgiven himself for the way he left her—and
fifteen years later, he's determined to win her back.

Though the attraction is still there, Helena is hesitant
to get involved. Nick left her once...what's to stop
him from doing it again?

HM38964

ATHENA FORCE

Heart-pounding romance and thrilling adventure.

A deadly masquerade

As an undercover asset for the FBI, mafia princess Sasha Bracciali can deceive and improvise at a moment's notice. But when she's cut off from everything she knows, including her FBI-agent lover, Sasha realizes her deceptions have masked a painful truth: she doesn't know whom to trust. If she doesn't figure it out quickly, her most ambitious charade will also be her last.

Look for

CHARADE
by *Kate Donovan*

Available in October wherever you buy books.

www.eHarlequin.com

AF38974

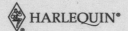

HARLEQUIN®

INTRIGUE®

COMING NEXT MONTH

#1017 RETURN OF THE WARRIOR by Rebecca York
43 Light Street
When the spirit of an ancient warrior takes over Luke McMillan's body, can Luke control his new urges long enough to save Sidney Weston's life—and free this trapped soul, *without* dying?

#1018 HIS NEW NANNY by Carla Cassidy
Amanda Rockport traveled to Louisiana to caretake for Sawyer Bennett's child, not expecting to discover a makeshift family that needed her to hold it together as their secrets pulled them apart.

#1019 TEXAS GUN SMOKE by Joanna Wayne
Four Brothers of Colts Run Cross
Jaclyn McGregor has a traumatic past she no longer remembers. But when ranching baron Bart Collingsworth rescues her from a car accident, he's not buying her story—but it won't stop him from getting mixed up with a woman who truly needs him.

#1020 IN THE DEAD OF NIGHT by Linda Castillo
Chief of Police Nick Tyson isn't the least bit happy to revisit the event that left his own family shattered. But there's no way Nick can turn the other cheek when someone tries to take Sara Douglas's life—even if he hoped he'd never see her again.

#1021 A FATHER'S SACRIFICE by Mallory Kane
Neurosurgeon Dylan Stryker will sacrifice anything, even his own life, to give his toddler son the ability to walk. But it will take FBI agent Natasha Rudolph to face her worst fear to save the man she's falling in love with and the little boy who has already captured her heart.

#1022 ROYAL HEIR by Alice Sharpe
William Chastain and Julia Sheridan lead a desperate hunt to rescue William's son—and restore his royal heritage.

www.eHarlequin.com

HICNM0907